I0720391

# The Derbyshire Set ~ Book 4

## Regency Historical Romance

# The Counts Impetuous Seduction

## Arietta Richmond

**Dreamstone Publishing © 2016**

**www.dreamstonepublishing.com**



ISBN-13:   978-1-925165-65-4

# Books by Arietta Richmond

## His Majesty's Hounds

Claiming the Heart of a Duke

Intriguing the Viscount

Giving a Heart of Lace (a prequel to Winning the Merchant Earl)

Being Lady Harriet's Hero

Enchanting the Duke (coming soon)

Redeeming the Marquess (coming soon)

Healing Lord Barton (coming soon)

Winning the Merchant Earl (coming soon)

Loving the Bitter Baron (coming soon)

Rescuing the Countess (coming soon)

Attracting the Spymaster (coming soon)

## The Derbyshire Set

A Gift of Love (Prequel short story)

A Devil's Bargain (Prequel short story - coming soon)

The Earl's Unexpected Bride

The Captain's Compromised Heiress

The Viscount's Unsuitable Affair

The Count's Impetuous Seduction

The Rake's Unlikely Redemption

The Marquess' Scandalous Mistress

A Remembered Face (Bonus short story – coming soon)

The Marchioness' Second Chance (coming soon)

A Viscount's Reluctant Passion (coming soon)

Lady Theodora's Christmas Wish

The Duke's Improper Love (coming soon)

## Other Books

The Scottish Governess (coming soon)

The Earl's Reluctant Fiancée (coming soon)

The Crew of the Seadragon's Soul Series, (coming soon - a set of 10 linked novels)

ARIETTA RICHMOND

# Dedication

For everyone who had the grace to be patient while this book, and the ones before and after it, were coming into existence, who provided cups of tea, and food, when the writing would not let me go, and endured countless times being asked for opinions.

For the readers coming to know these characters well, and who inspire me to continue, by buying my books!

And for all the writers of Regency Historical Romance, whose books I read, who inspired me to write in this fascinating period.

ARIETTA RICHMOND

# Chapter One

Charlotte cast her eyes around the church, looking for Don Diego. With a dismayed sigh she realised that he did not appear to be among the guests, here for her sister's wedding. She stifled her sigh so as not to alert the other guests to her desperation. For weeks this had been the only date on her mind, the only day that she could focus on, whenever she looked at a calendar or glanced ahead in her diary. It was today, the twelfth of June 1817, the day that she would be reunited with her Don, yet it had come and he did not seem to be here.

It was almost too much. This might be the greatest day of her sister's life, but she was not sure she could bear it. Risking ruination, she thought about getting up and running out, finding a quiet spot in the shadow of a yew tree, or beside a grave, in which to cry her eyes out.

Despite all of the affection that she had towards her older sister, who was marrying her handsome captain, the joy of the occasion dissipated. It seemed as if all she could imagine of life from here on was struggle and pain.

She had poured over Diego's short note obsessively, ever since it was delivered to her, shortly after he had left for London.. Every word had been scrutinized, every syllable picked apart, ever stroke of his pen analysed for signs of his true feelings. He had addressed her as 'My Lady' but then signed off as 'ever yours', a strange clash of formality that could probably be attributed to him being a foreigner.

Likewise, he had said that he was 'eagerly awaiting the chance to see you again', but in her infatuated haze she could not allow herself to believe that this was an entirely sincere expression. Did he mean it, or was he merely being polite?

Was he really eager about her, or merely about another occasion in the social calendar? It was impossible, trying to start a love affair with a letter, yet in her head it was almost as if she had done everything in her power to do so. She closed her eyes to go to sleep every night and he was there, holding out his hand to her, smiling at her on the dance floor, his flamboyant Latin attire glistening in the candlelight. But he was not here, and that seemed to be all that mattered for the present.

Charlotte, trying very hard to look demure and entirely focused on the wedding proceedings, still desperately craned her neck, trying to get a look around the columns of the church.

It was possible, if unlikely, that she had not seem him entering, and that he was in one of the many nooks and crannies around Tideswell Parish Church that was not visible from where she was sitting, in pride of place beside her mother and father, in the first rank of pews. As her eyes darted around the room they met the gaze of many strangers, and many more relations and friends of the family. There was Lady Staveley, looking fatter by the year, and Miss Henrietta Elmton, still without a husband even after her thirtieth year.

They all looked back at her curiously, presumably wondering why on earth Blanchette's sister was behaving in such a distracted and unseemly fashion on the day of her sister's wedding.

All the faces seemed familiar to her, until suddenly, her eye settled on one face, handsome, distinct, masculine, that she had never seen before but immediately wanted to go on seeing, for as long as she dared.

He was seated near the back of the modestly sized church, and seemed to be alone, or as good as. The moment she spotted him she was surprised that she had not noticed him earlier, owing to the fact that he seemed almost to dominate his entire pew, so bright was his shock of red-brown hair.

He seemed, from his bearing, his ferociously intense gaze and the half smile that curled the corner of his lip, to be in command of all his surrounds, with that easy swagger that comes to many sons of the nobility.

He wore a dark green coat and a richly embroidered waistcoat, topped by a crisp white cravat, all finely tailored, all enhancing his appearance of nobility and confidence.

Charlotte was seated some distance from him, but she could see that he had the most incredible green eyes, of a brighter green than she had ever before seen, looking intently forward, towards the ceremony going on at the front of the church. She could not quite understand it, but she was for a few moments at least, distracted from thoughts of Don Diego, and focussed instead on this mysterious, dashing young man whom she had never seen before. Ignoring all laws of etiquette and sisterly decency, she turned to her mother.

"Mother" she whispered, as loudly as she dared "-who is that fellow near the back of the church with the reddish brown hair? I don't believe I have ever laid eyes on him..."

"Shush girl!" her mother hissed back "- have you no notion of decency? This is your sister's wedding!" and Charlotte noticed Captain Westbury, looking remarkably handsome in his full parade uniform of the guards, twitch slightly at the sound of muttering behind him. The threat of the soldier's fury, and the prospect of her shame-faced apologies to Blanche at the reception party, was enough to silence her.

Her mother however, to her immense surprise, had turned around to follow up her interest, despite her earlier recrimination. She saw her look carefully behind, scouring the banks of seats for a sight of the man her daughter had just mentioned.

"I see who you mean" Lady Derbyshire said, directly into Charlotte's ear, with practised discretion. "I believe that is the Marquess Hemsbridge, from down in Somerset. You'll have to ask your father if you want more detail; he invited the fellow". Charlotte's interest was piqued.

A Marquess? And yet he looked so young and full of life and energy, to have already come into possession of a great estate and title was most impressive to the impressionable young girl of twenty. Charlotte leaned in towards her mother, and almost as privately, whispered:

"He's rather handsome isn't he?"

"Coarse girl!" came the immediate response, Lady Derbyshire's shock barely contained by her whisper. "- to speak of such things on an occasion like this!" Then however, her mother glanced around for another quick peak at Hemsbridge.

"Between you and me however..." Charlotte barely repressed a giggle at her mother's tone, which would have been especially embarrassing had it escaped. At the front of the church, the Bishop of Derby was just working his way towards the vows. "... I should have to say I echo your sentiment. Don't you dare disclose that to your father however!" They shared a second's grin, and returned to facing the front.

"If any person present..." the Bishop droned on in his reedy, pious voice "... knows of any reason why these two may not be joined together in Holy Matrimony, may he speak now, or else, forever hold his peace." An awestruck silence descended on the room. Many here had been present at Blanche's abortive wedding a few short months ago, and instinctively, they feared a repeat performance.

This time, however, (perhaps owing in part to the absence of one Mr. James Blackwood) nobody spoke up, Captain Westbury held his ground, and Blanche was able to quickly turn the fearful expression with which she had regarded the room into one of happiness and security.

"Lady Blanchette Cavendish, do you take this man, Captain Henry Westbury..." the bishop carried on, and for the first time that day, with her sister finally tying the knot, Don Diego somewhere in England, hopefully pining after her, and that handsome stranger Hemsbridge seated at the back of the church, Charlotte Cavendish felt nothing but happiness at being alive.

Outside, the congregation greeted the happy couple with cheers, a few tears, and showers of flower petals. Bells pealed, and despite their friendly rivalry for the attentions of desirable men like Henry Westbury, which had persisted throughout their adolescence, Charlotte was swept along in all the good feeling, and felt overjoyed for her sister. Captain Westbury turned to face the crowd for a moment, with Blanche in his arms, and cried out in his commanding, military voice:

"My Lords, Ladies, and Gentlemen - to Amfield!" the guests cheered once again at this, and all at once set about the rather arduous process of each collecting their maids and footmen and making for their carriages. There was to be a great ball this evening, in celebration of the wedding, at a cost which Lord Derbyshire had winced at on principle, and then happily paid.

The servants at Amfield had been in a frenzy of preparation to ensure that only the best was provided. Tomorrow, after the celebration was complete, Blanche and her Henry would set off for Italy, for a leisurely and protracted honeymoon which would presumably involve the delicate business of producing an heir...

In the press of bodies that had assembled along the small churchyard path, Charlotte found herself suddenly and unexpectedly separated from her parents, with whom she would be riding back to her house. Momentarily panicked, she tried to raise her small frame upwards to spot them amongst the crowds, but could not. She was considering calling out when suddenly, as she turned, looking for them, she found herself face to face, indeed somewhat closer than that, in the crush of people, with Lord Hemsbridge, the man whose eye she had met inside the church, looking even more impressive seen close up, as he strode assertively towards his carriage.

"I beg your pardon, my Lord!" Charlotte could not help but cry out at once. Fixed by his powerful, green gaze, she was suddenly frozen in place, her awareness of the crowd around her fading away, and she felt an unfortunate blush creeping up the back of her neck. He was undoubtedly handsome; she only hoped that he would not notice her sudden redness, or if he did, that he would be enough of a gentleman to pretend he had not, and therefore not embarrass her completely.

"Please, the fault was entirely mine" he said in a crisp voice that did not sound used to waiting around or indulging in idle chit chat. He gazed at her for a moment, as if he were looking for something in her face, in the depths of her pale blue eyes or the slight kink in her fair hair.

His eyes narrowed contemplatively, and they shared a silent moment of communication, seeming to say all that needed to be said of the attraction that instantly existed between them, with their eyes and faces.

"Forgive me" he said, injecting a little more warmth into his tone of voice "- I don't believe we've been introduced" he placed his hand on his broad, toned breast, and offered a slight bow. "I am Marquess Hemsbridge; I have journeyed up from Somerset at the behest of the Earl of Derbyshire. My attendance had been a mere formality but now that I see that with such fair company..." he maintained his piercing gaze, even as he stopped to kiss Charlotte's hand. She felt a little flutter, somewhere deep inside her. For a moment Don Diego seemed to be but a passing fancy. "- I can see that the trip was not in vain. What is your name, my Lady?"

"I am Lady Charlotte Cavendish" Charlotte replied, trying to be coy and reserved, as Blanche would be when confronted by a handsome gentleman. "I am the younger daughter of the aforementioned Earl, and also have the privilege of being sister to the bride."

"You are Lady Blanchette's sister?" Hemsbridge said, promptly. "- and there was I convinced that the fairest of the famous Cavendish sisters had already been wed. It is a bounteous pleasure to make your acquaintance."

"The pleasure is undoubtedly mutual, sir" said Charlotte, with a pleasantly flirtatious nod that concealed the complex and powerful feelings bubbling up inside of her. She still felt for her Don, yearned for him even, and yet this man had stirred something in her as well, something irrepressible, and impossible to ignore.

Was love always this difficult, she felt like exclaiming? "- I trust you shall be joining us at Amfield House for the subsequent celebrations?"

"Undoubtedly" he replied, not wasting a single breath. "I had wondered whether such an attendance would be worth my while, but I can see now…" he regarded her conspiratorially. She knew that dark look some gentlemen liked to throw out. Charlotte was used to watching other girls receive it, bat their eyelashes and glance away from it tenderly, and it was quite a thrill to finally be on the receiving end. What great mysteries those green eyes concealed!

"… that it would be quite a pleasure."

"Indeed, my Lord. I must now re-join my carriage; however, I trust you shall have a safe and comfortable passage through the Peaks."

"As do I." He replied. "Safe and comfortable indeed." They looked at each other, the one contemplating the other, imagining all manner of carnal possibilities in the silent and private parts of their minds. And then without another word, Charlotte turned, and hurried to re-join her family for the ride back to Amfield House.

# Chapter Three

Charlotte did not see Lord Hemsbridge for a while at Amfield. The ride over from Tideswell took over an hour, and many of the carriages chose to take it very slowly, their footmen and horses being unused to this rough, Derbyshire country. The bumping and the jolting, along some of the gravelly roads, was quite intense, and the sensation of it proved enough to remind Charlotte quite abruptly of her feelings.

An anxiety concerning Don Diego enveloped her suddenly, waxing and waning in concert with a deep desire to be with him, to be held by the dashing Argentine, to dance along to his unorthodox Latin rhythms and kiss him under the lights of another great ball. Whether he would be there or not she could not say, though she took some comfort from that fact that her newfound acquaintance with Lord Hemsbridge would guarantee that, should the Don not appear, she would at least be entertained.

She settled back, admiring the scenery about her, that she called home. She was used to this hilly serenity, the smell of wet bracken and dewy heather, the sight of screes tumbling down hillsides and little slate cottages clinging to the edges of valleys. It was undeniably beautiful, and distracted her pleasantly for a few moments.

At the great meal they had laid out in the dining hall, Charlotte found herself seated not, as she secretly desired but knew was unlikely to pass, by Lord Hemsbridge, but between her uncle Herbert, Viscount Frome, her father's youngest brother, and his wife, Lady Frome. Charlotte had always found Lady Frome's company horrifyingly dull, and was now distracting herself as often as she dared, both from the conversation around her and the Turtle soup that she was sloshing about in her bowl, by glancing towards Marquess Hemsbridge's end of the table.

"- and of course, then we had to dismiss our Housekeeper, Mrs. Barnstable" said Lady Frome, in a voice that was at once, loud and remarkably uninspiring. Charlotte nodded, but could not summon enough enthusiasm to look up from the thick brown soup upon the table.

"We'd had her on for a full two-score years, but regrettably, if one's servants forget the manner in which one is accustomed to taking cream tea, then one has no option but to do the decent thing, for their sakes, as much as one's own." Charlotte feigned another nod, but was instantly distracted from her aunt's conversation (and from the tiny pang of compassion she felt towards the unfortunate Mrs. Barnstable) by a second's eye contact with Hemsbridge.

He was looking over towards her, there was no denying it, and for an instant her eyes met his in an intoxicating communication of desire. She found her heart beating faster, and suddenly felt that the room was entirely too warm. She felt herself drowning in those green eyes, and seemed unable to look away. Then, as if they had been choreographed to do so and practised beforehand, like courting swans they whipped their necks to the side and looked away, not allowing the other too much certainty, sustaining the mystery of their passions.

"… I instructed our head groundskeeper, Smithers, to put in some rhododendrons for this particular season, but he appears to have rather under-done it, by my estimation. I was hoping to be able to promenade in a sea of blooming pink, but it seems, I shall have to make do with little more than a boating pond's worth. Most unfortunate." Lady Frome was one of those upper-class ladies whose conversation is limited, and who, it seems, after their sons have gone off to make their fortunes and their daughters have all been wed, have nothing else to talk about but the domestic affairs of their household.

She could hold forth for hours on end about nothing more than the personalities and predilections, successes and failures of her staff, none of whom Charlotte had ever even met. It was enough to drive any clever young girl to distraction, and Charlotte was more than happy to be distracted by Hemsbridge, that shock of ruddy masculinity on the other side of the room. She was displeased to note however, as she gazed towards him for what had to be the dozenth time, that he appeared to be getting along rather well with a pretty young lady seated to his right.

Charlotte almost clanked her spoon against her soup bowl in momentary frustration. '*If only*' she thought, '*someone had seen fit to seat me next to him instead!*'

"I am very seriously considering replacing him" Lady Frome blathered on, seeming neither to know nor care how little Charlotte was bothered by her relations with her servants.

"Only last year, Herbert here was nearly killed by a stray rake he'd left lying around by the veranda, weren't you Herbert?"

"What?" Uncle Herbert replied, seemingly half-asleep. "Oh yes, yes, terrible" and he returned instantly to his soup.

Later on in the ball room, the real business of the evening began.

For a short while the newlywed Blanche and the Captain circulated amongst the attendees, receiving congratulations, and chatting with everyone, as others milled about and talked also, giving the many young and unwed persons around the floor plenty of time to get acquainted with the objects of their desires (or their parents dynastic ambitions, depending on the people in question).

Finally the dancing began, with a waltz, and Charlotte looked on as Blanche and Henry swayed gently in each other's arms, and could not help but feel the small pang of an old jealousy aroused within her, despite her earlier joy in the church.

They were certainly a handsome couple, the very image of a prosperous and successful match, but, despite this, she suspected she was not alone in feeling quietly muted in her enthusiasm for the celebration of it.

To further compound any vicarious feelings of happiness, Charlotte also had to contend with both the ongoing absence of Don Diego, something which continued to give her occasional convulsions of dread in her heart, and in her stomach, which were not helped by the sight of the new object of her interest, Lord Hemsbridge, flirting gamely with a selection of the prettiest maidens in the room.

She noted, with barely suppressed displeasure, his apparent insatiability - no sooner had he charmed his way into the blushes and giggles of one girl, standing fanning herself and feeling very flattered on the edges of the ballroom, than he had moved on to the next. It was almost as if he seemed to enjoy the very process of it, finding attractive and impressionable young women, leading them to believe that perhaps they had engaged his affections, and then leaving them to stand alone, feeling jealous of his next target.

Having been in this sort of position before, Charlotte was silently reaching a point of desperation. Innumerable were the times that she had felt that she had made some meaningful connection with an attractive gentleman, only to have to watch him go off with some other, often prettier, or at least more demure, girl, while she sat on the side-lines and simmered in unladylike frustration.

Calamity struck, from Charlotte's point of view, at least, in the form of the pretty young miss he had been getting on with so handsomely at dinner. Having circulated through the fluttering crowd of young ladies, Marquess Hemsbridge had found himself at her side and they were soon talking once again.

The young lady was beaming great smiles, and fluttering her fan about her face as she looked at him, in a way that left Charlotte in doubt as to the fact that the young lady was experiencing a very particular sensation. Then they were taking to the dancefloor, the first of the unmarried couples to take up a dance.

This was unexpected, and there were a few raised eyebrows among the chaperones, though the suitability of the match and the timing of the dance, which was a harmless enough country reel, could not be faulted, so there was no need for a disruptive intervention. Charlotte was not alone in looking on with barely concealed pain and regret, as he pulled the young woman close at every opportunity the dance presented, and twirled her lithe young body about his lean strong frame with charm and grace.

She was so focussed on this action in the centre of the room she barely noticed Lady Frome come up close behind her, and make her first remark of the evening about a subject other than herself and her own domestic affairs...

"That's Lord Hemsbridge" she said quietly, presuming with good reason that her niece was unacquainted with the gentleman in question. "- the most eligible bachelor in our own county of Somerset, and a great many other places besides I should think..." her tone had changed considerably, moving beyond the drab barking of earlier, into a sultry hiss.

Charlotte suddenly felt more interested in her aunt than she ever had before, if only because she appeared to have some connection to this fascinating young gentleman in the centre of the room.

"Tell me, Lady Frome…" she said, imitating the voice of conspiracy her aunt had dropped into so deftly. "… does Lord Hemsbridge often come this far north in search of society?"

"Very rarely" Lady Frome replied

"I should think that few of the ladies present, being from Derbyshire and its surrounding shires, would have been previously acquainted with our handsome Marquess here. He is however, a regular at occasions of this ilk down in Somerset, and might I add…" she leaned a little closer, and Charlotte, still staring intently Hemsbridge, felt quite a quiver of fascination running through her, despite her better interests, the behaviour and thinking appropriate to a young maiden, and her infatuation with Don Diego

"… has often proved just as attractive to young ladies in that part of the kingdom as well."

"Is that so, my Lady?" Charlotte replied, playing along "I could have said earlier that I had no notion of what you are speaking of, though now you come to mention it, he does seem to have a certain charm about him."

"Undoubtedly. Young Miss Gaviston seems quite taken with him, although I have noticed in the past…" again Lady Frome leaned in closer, as if about to disclose some piece of insight too delicious to be shared with anyone else.

"- that Lord Hemsbridge likes to save dancing with the real object of his affections, until later in the evening".

"What a queer strategy" said Charlotte, immediately swelling once again with an ecstasy of hope.

"You might think it so" said Lady Frome "- but in my, not inconsiderable, experience of the ways of society, it is common for gentlemen to arouse the interest of the onlooker they truly desire, by feigning an attraction to another". Charlotte nodded in response.

She had heard of such things, though she had always considered herself a poor judge of such ploys and dynamics. It seemed now, with the assistance of her grossly underestimated aunt, that she was growing into a newer, deeper understanding of the workings of these affairs.

"It is often prudent, in my judgement" continued the old aunt, wittier than ever "- for young ladies who wish to arouse the interest of a particular gentleman to opt for a similar angle of approach."

"Very interesting, my Lady." Charlotte replied, feigning innocence "- and what might such tactics entail?"

"Well... speaking hypothetically of course, one could always, for example, court the attentions of another gentleman, lesser in one's own esteem, but a suitable dancing or conversational partner to allow oneself to be as it were..." she paused over her wording for just a second "- more widely noticed?" They shared a knowing smile, saying with their eyes and the curls of their mouths what they dare not pronounce too explicitly.

"A very interesting insight, Lady Frome." said Charlotte, breaking the moment of bonding between niece and aunt. "Very interesting indeed." And with that, Lady Frome shrunk back slightly, giving Charlotte the space she needed to do as the situation required.

She hesitated a moment, considering her options, scanning the room for a gentleman suitable to her purpose. After a moment, she fixed her sights on William Banbury, a good-natured and not unattractive fellow, whom she and her family had known, vaguely, since she was a girl.

Charlotte had no particular interest in him as a potential match, but she liked him well enough, and knew that to speak and dance with him would be considered far from beneath her, even as the prettier than average daughter of an Earl.

Subtly, wordlessly, she took up her fan and fluttered it in front of her face, smiling slightly, but generally avoiding eye contact, fixing the general axis of her body towards young Banbury, pointing the toe end of her foot at him. She took it all in as he registered her gesture, at first with surprise, then with gladness, and then finally with a growing confidence.

'*Good grief!*' she thought, as he began to move, purposefully but not without a hint of caution, in her direction '-*this flirting business really is painfully easy when you fully commit yourself to it!*' He approached her, and she put on a look she had seen Blanche and others use with great success over the years, bashful, even forlorn, like the first sight of a rosebud on a cool spring morning.

Lady Charlotte he said, trying to conceal his evident shyness and not inconsiderable surprise. He had slender well-proportioned features, and well-set, dark compelling eyes beneath deep mahogany coloured hair. He was not exceptionally tall but, Charlotte considered, he was a decent enough-looking fellow.

"I feel that as childhood friends, and considering the immense honour this occasion brings to your great family, it would be appropriate for us to dance – that is, if you have not already committed this dance to another ?" he extended his hand firmly, and, after a moment's pause to act out consideration, she daintily placed her hand in his.

"Sir is most kind" she said, still barely meeting his eyes. '*Much more of this*', she thought, '*- and I'll be the most sought after young lady in all of England!*'

"I do have this dance free, and I shall happily accept your invitation."

They shared a warm, friendly sort of a smile, and proceeded onto the dance floor, there to absorb the glances of all assembled, including, Charlotte noted with glee, the devilishly handsome Lord Hemsbridge.

# Chapter Four

Charlotte and Banbury danced together, precipitating a rush of couples to the ballroom floor as the next dance began. The musicians picked up their volume and tempo accordingly, and so the whole room seemed to be in thrall to music and motion, and to the flirtatious movements of the young and unwed.

Many of the older chaperones looked on aghast, rueing the loss of standards since their day, the strange new fashions in clothing and dance, and the apparent wanton abandon of their sons and daughters, nieces, nephews and grandchildren.

They accepted that it was a necessary function of society that young people must be allowed some small liberty to fraternize as they wished, but that did not make them at all happy about it!

Ultimately most of them would have been far happier if all of the marriages that were legally and morally necessary to the perpetuation of the aristocracy could have been worked out in advance, in private, between those who actually paid the dowries and organised the ceremonies, i.e. them. All of this gyrating and encircling, fluttering of fans and impenetrable courtship ritual was tiring, and time-consuming, and encouraged the wrong sort of thoughts, the wrong types of liaisons.

There was some opportunity for conversation as Charlotte danced with Banbury, but though it was pleasant enough, it did not provoke her to any deeper interest in him. They spoke of the fates of various relatives and acquaintances, of Blanche and Westbury's wedding, Stanningfield and his governess, now wife, and of the general affairs of society. Having been acquainted since infancy, the two were comfortable in one another's presence, with ample subjects of polite engagement between them, but little to arouse passionate discourse on anything.

In any case, Charlotte was distracted by Hemsbridge, whom, she noted with pleasure, had glanced in her direction on more than one occasion, in spite of his preoccupation with another partner. On one such occasion their eyes met for just a second, long enough, however, for him to throw her a little smile, and the ghostly outline of a nod. A jolt of pleasure ran through her at this, but she kept her attention on her own partner so as not to appear churlish or over-eager.

She was just collecting a small measure of punch from one of the staff when the little plan she had hatched, in inference, with her aunt, came to a sort of fruition.

Hemsbridge, newly liberated from the pretty Miss Gaviston, approached her unexpectedly, almost startling her for a moment. Charlotte was mere fractions of a second from throwing away all of her good work with a shocked outburst, but maintained her composure and remembered to remain lady-like and a little cool, as she had before.

"Lady Charlotte" he said boldly "- I trust your perambulation upon the dance floor was smoother than your coach trip over the Derbyshire peaks."

"It undoubtedly was, sir" she replied, wielding a fan in one hand and a glass of punch in the other. She was quite well-equipped for her sally forth onto the battlefields of the heart. "- considerably smoother, as one would hope of such an experience."

"Indeed, I must confess, I too found the experience more pleasurable. I am unused to the topographical dramas of your northern county, but found the scenery as worthy of note as I had been told.  And since my arrival here I have found the partnership of Miss Gaviston to be rather amenable."

Whilst he had spoken to many of the young ladies present, he had, so far, only danced with Miss Gaviston.  Charlotte carefully considered her reply.

"She is a fair young woman, certainly" Charlotte said "-and I can perceive her appeal to a gentleman" he looked at her with interest, hanging on her words, willing her to meet his gaze, which she would only fleetingly do, "-though many would consider it to be not only improperly scandalous to lean too heavily upon a single dancing partner at an evening of society, but quite rash at best."

"Indeed some would" he said "-and what measure would you suggest as a remedy for my single-partner affliction?"

"Why is it not obvious, My Lord?" she bandied back, giggling slightly. "It is necessary to find another partner! Perhaps, dare I add…" and at last she looked at him, straight into those fascinating green eyes she had been craving for hours, "- a more suitable one, at that." He smiled at her knowingly, raising his right eyebrow just a little.

"In that case, Lady Charlotte" he said "would you do me the honour, of expanding my social horizons?" he extended his hand with greater firmness and confidence that Banbury, and after a moment of lingering anticipation, she took it gladly.

"I shall sir" she replied. "I shall indeed."

# Chapter Five

They danced for a span of time, which felt at once like the passage of a few seconds and an eternity of excitement and ruction. Lord Hemsbridge was truly a superb dancer, perhaps the best Charlotte had ever been with (except of course, for her beloved Don, not by any means banished from her thoughts, but at least in the background, behind this dashing young Lord for the moment). The experience to which Lady Frome had alluded shone through, and despite her better instincts, on one level she was pleased that she was the latest in a long succession of dance partners for him.

It gave her a sense of him, of his strength, of being at the heart of some great centre of energy and attraction, and it was a good feeling. She felt it, running up the inside of her leg, emanating inwards and out, pulsing in time to the music and making her conscious of the layers of petticoat beneath her frock.

What an exciting period of life this was for her! Truly, despite the very short time that had elapsed since she had first caught sight of Don Diego, she could never go back to her earlier self. It was almost as if (and the very thought itself filled her up to the top both with excitement and dread) she was moving away from her girlhood, and rapidly becoming a woman.

Had she been asked subsequently, she could not have said how long they danced together. It had been dark when they started, so the sky outside, visible through the great windows of the Amfield ballroom, gave her no clues. There was no clock in the ballroom either, her mother having declared that "it does not do to have reminder of one's mortality present at an occasion where young ladies and gentlemen are to meet". Charlotte felt now as if she had a stronger idea of what Lady Cavendish had been getting at.

It was a period long enough for them to start to tire. Charlotte was unused to intense bouts of physical exercise, and even Lord Hemsbridge, despite the sporting interests his athletic physique betrayed, started to seem a little overheated after a while, country dances being rather energetic in style. They retired to a quiet corner of the room to converse.

"Your dancing is well-practiced, My Lord." Charlotte said, throwing him a small compliment for the first time "-I have gained the impression that occasions such as this are not new to you?"

"Indeed not, Lady Charlotte" he replied "- though it is rare indeed in Somerset shire to find so many eminently attractive possible partners in a single room."

"So many my Lord?" she said, playfully "why then you shall be quite worn out by the end of your evening's exertions."

"It is something to hope for, I suppose" he said, unflappable. "Although I must confess, my mortal limitations may compel me to restrict myself somewhat. Perhaps to only two, scandalous as that may be."

"Is that so, sir? In that case you have aroused my interest enough for me to enquire, which of your two partners you intend to pass the remainder of the evening with?"

He paused, throwing her a wry smile.

She could tell in that moment that she had not, as she had so many times in the past, overstepped the mark and transgressed the role normally expected of a young lady, and that in fact, she had him, had entranced him, was pulling him towards her, as she knew now she desired.

Oh, it was so devious, and yet so enjoyable at the same time! Was this the gift of Don Diego's Latin spontaneity that had spurred her on to these feats of coyness and flirtation?

"The answer to that intriguing little quandary" he replied, his smooth, full lips close to her face, "- may be obtained via a walk in the grounds, and further conversation - if you would not think it wildly improper for me to make such a proposition in your own family's house?"

"No sir, not improper" she said, knowing all the while that it was exactly that – quite improper indeed.  She pulled away from him just to see how far he was willing to go in her pursuit, before she continued speaking.

"Perhaps a little bold, but then that has always been a quality of Englishmen has it not? Especially those with excellent breeding. Perhaps I shall show you our Italian garden, it will still be quite visible in the moonlight. You may follow, if you wish."

With a flutter of her eyelids and a handsome suitor in tow, Charlotte stole out unnoticed, but not unpursued.

Out in the Italian garden, the scent of herbs and flowers was strong. With the coming of the summer months everything was in full bloom and emitting pungent, evocative scents that stirred the senses. A bank of rosemary and lavender was especially aromatic, the rich scent of the latter mingling with the herbaceous power of the former. It evoked in Charlotte a sense of opening up, a feeling of natural forces beyond her control and of distant, exotic sensations coming ever closer. Strolling arm in arm with Hemsbridge between the marble statuary and under the aegis of the arboretum, the ambience became almost over-powering, and she felt an immense sense of stimulation.

"Your family's recreation of the gardens of Verona, or is it Genoa, is most evocative, My Lady" said Hemsbridge, with compelling firmness. "- I feel almost as if I were back in that fine country."

"You have journeyed in Italy, My Lord?" asked Charlotte, intrigued.

"Certainly. Before my late father passed away, leaving me the honour of my present title, he took me on something of a tour of that ancient and serene land. We visited many of the centres of classical learning and literature."

"Did you indeed? And what impression did they make upon you?"

"A most excellent one. I have, myself, installed an Italian-style drawing room back at my house in Somerset. I had aimed to imitate the style of some of the gardens that I saw, as well, but alas I have yet to find the time to implement my designs."

"That is a shame."

"Certainly, though Amfield appears to have more than compensated for my prevarications." He gestured to indicate their handsome surroundings.  Charlotte found that she was perceiving the gardens with fresh eyes, as if through the company of this dashing young gentleman she herself was experiencing exotic lands, new ideas, and novel notions of how to live and behave. An interesting echo of how she had felt with Don Diego....

The garden that she had grown up with suddenly seemed like it had layers of additional depth to be discovered, adventures tucked away in its gilded features and herbaceous borders.

"- and what of Italian ladies, My Lord?" she said to him, stepping gaily ahead of him to arouse his energy and interest, almost feeling his eyes upon her trim shape as she walked.

"So often I hear gentlemen compare them favourably to those of the northern climes."

He stood firm and still for a moment, and their eyes met. There was a new intensity to his entire bearing as he considered what had been said, as his mind wandered, as she had wished it to, to notions of beauty, and carnal desire. The communion they were enacting with their eyes was intoxicating, and though her mind was not set on keeping track of it or diagnosing herself, Charlotte felt herself reacting bodily, hot and wet, and tingling all over, even before there had been any close contact between them. The Don was entirely banished from her thoughts, for the moment.

"They're not so bad, I suppose" he responded, with a distinct and deliberate erection of his right eyebrow up towards his russet fringe, "-but give me a beautiful English rose over an Italian thistle any day" and then without question, pause or further thought they were kissing each other, initially with an uncontrollable forcefulness, as if each was afraid the other might pull away on the moment, but then, as quickly as it had begun, it became softer and more sensual, in a rhythm that imitated their dance from earlier in the ball.

His hands slid to her sides and he grasped her, pulling her close, until she could feel him against her, the pulsations of their two bodies, breasts and hearts and other, rather obvious, parts, all throbbing together through their fine garments, as a wave of arousal ran through them.

It was immediately obvious to her that he was as excited by having her in his arms as she was by being there.

His touch was heated, and somehow, through the layers of cloth, still manged to make her feel as if his fingers touched her skin directly.  It was strong, but also practised, attuned to her needs, in command of the sensations that he conjured deep within her. Their tongues met like courting birds, twittering and fluttering, coming together and then pulling apart with a natural compulsion that did not need thought to function.

For the first time since her early childhood, Charlotte felt as if she was able to switch off her conscious mind, to stop thinking and planning and worrying over ideas and notions, and to simply be, mind and body and heart all acting as one.

Without warning, Hemsbridge's gently sensual approach came to an abrupt end, his desire apparently completely overcoming his manners. He grasped her back, hands straying close to her buttocks, still sending shivers through her with every insistent touch, but now more assertive than tender. She could feel his fingers seeming to claw into her, grasping for her body through the cloth as his tongue began to thrust hard into her mouth, penetrating her innocence, breaking up the dance and forcing its way deeper into her mouth.

Her feelings of excited pleasure had not entirely disappeared, but they had been stoked to an intensity she did not want, had not given her consent to, and did not know how to deal with. The intensity frightened her, so sudden a transition it had been, as he moved from gentle kisses to hungry desire. Their teeth clashed in a moment that brought everything back, down from up in the clouds to an earthy, raw sensation which Charlotte was not at all sure she liked.

Don Diego, who she had promised herself to as she lay alone, in the bitter watches of the night, came flooding back into her thoughts, as if speeding to her rescue on a glorious white charger. Had this whole thing been a terrible mistake? Had she surrendered herself to lust in the manner she had been warned of, but never previously had to fear?  How could she extricate herself from this situation?  The thoughts rushed through her mind as Hemsbridge continued his assault on her person.

He had, with a skill that spoke of practice, gathered up her skirts with one hand, as he held her hard against him with the other. She gasped against his demanding mouth as he took advantage of her helpless position, and slid his fingers past her petticoats and drawers, to touch her most intimate flesh.  The touch of his fingers there shocked her utterly. With an acute sensation that was neither pleasant nor comfortable, like falling on to the arm of a chair by mistake, Hemsbridge's hand went too far, too fast.

In a single practiced motion, which she feared he had done many times before, with many other unassuming maidens, his fingers thrust at her, rapidly, forcefully, thrusting into and against her flesh in a way that she was unable to take in, unable to deal with,perverting the pleasant sensations she had been so enjoying and turning them into a numbness, and a nausea.

She was stunned, unsure of what to do, had not, indeed, even known that a gentleman might do such a thing.  The sensation was strange, and she suspected, could even be pleasant in the right circumstances, but most definitely was not, like this.

She squirmed, helplessly, trying to move away from the touch, but he apparently interpreted her movements as indicative of enjoyment.

He continued to kiss at her, nipping and biting at her neck, then returning to a deep and aggressive kiss, and though her arms remained fixed to him she now wished to pull away, and for her suitor to desist. Charlotte pushed against his chest, hard, but to no avail.  She tore her mouth from his and turned her head to the side, taking breath to speak.

"Sir, I think this most improvident" she at last managed to say, pulling away from him "- indeed, I might say, it is not entirely appropriate behaviour for a gentleman, should we be discovered like this, there would be terrible repercussions! I am a maiden!" Hemsbridge did not remove his hand from beneath her skirts, and his finger still moved, almost lazily against her, but he did stop kissing her.  The sensations that his hand created confused her, made her feel shaky, and somewhat desperate, especially as his other hand still held her hard against his body, and she could feel, most distinctly, through their clothes, the hard evidence of his unsated desire.

"Well…" he said, in tone of voice that she had previously considered rather charming, but could now only perceive as malicious "- there has to be a first time for everything, my dear. I had felt sure, from your flirtatious manner, and willingness to walk in the gardens, that you were rather expecting some activity of this nature. It would seem that I am mistaken. Or am I? Do you protest for propriety's sake, but truly wish for more?"

He leaned in further, insisting with a full-bodied force that they continue. His hand began to move again, faster, and harder, as he brushed his lips over hers, resuming his kiss.

For a moment she allowed him to kiss her again, because his kiss was soft and his face was still the same handsome countenance that had so impressed itself on her imagination in the church.

Swiftly she felt the need to pull away again, as the kiss became harsher, and the uninvited activities of his hand intensified again. She found herself rapidly losing all sense of pleasure, leaving only the sensation of being violated, and invaded. She wrenched herself from his grasp, stepping rapidly backwards away from the reach of his embrace, and nearly tripped on the edge of her petticoats as her skirts tumbled back into place.

"You may consider true propriety old-fashioned, sir, but it is not to me. I am an innocent in the affairs of the heart, and certainly in those of the flesh. I think you would do well to consider my honour, and for that matter, your own."

He made to lunge for her again, the predator eyeing up its prey, his heated desire evident in his eyes, but then, in the passing of a single second his eyes changed, and he stepped back.

The hungry look that had overcome him was replaced by one of sympathy, so fast that one might almost feel one had imagined it, and his hands, which had been tense like claws, retracted and softened once again, and his posture relaxed into that of a gentleman, rather than a caddish seducer.

Her heart quickly softened again, as she realised that, for the moment at least, she was safe from harm.

"I am aghast" he said "- please, accept my sincere apologies for my conduct, it was as if some demon possessed me."

"The demon of lust, my Lord" Charlotte replied, remaining on guard "- a troublingly common phantom often to be found in the souls of young men. I cannot blame you too harshly for falling prey to it, but please..." and she turned away, and started instinctively to head back towards Amfield House.

"... do not follow me, it is for the best if I re-join the party at once, and we do not speak again this evening."

Not giving herself time to think about what had happened, she walked rapidly back towards the house – there would be time to think about it later, when she was safely alone.

# Chapter Seven

Charlotte slept little that night. Thoughts and concerns consumed her, new anxieties, which she had no previous experience to help her make sense of, and which she could therefore not fathom. Had she been right to run away from Hemsbridge? What force of passion had moved him, and should she consider it a privilege to be so intensely desired by so handsome and eligible a suitor? What was the nature of the dread and confusion that she had felt at his touch, and at the vigorous insistence of his hands and tongue?

And how did Don Diego fit into all of this? Would he be in attendance at the party, as he had promised in his letter, or had he other, more pressing concerns? And what, if anything, did that say of his feelings for her? It was all too much to bear, she tossed and turned in bed for hours, struggling, sweating, desperate to know more and yet conscious of a nagging sense of dread.

She did not join the other guests for breakfast, but instead sat and took a simple meal of bread and butter in her room, as she often did when she was not feeling much inclined to engage in conversation. The servants were co-operative; they knew her quiet and often withdrawn habits, and her young maid Mary in particular, with whom Charlotte had something of a rapport, was very happy to serve her bread and offer a comforting smile.

"I'm sure that whatever's troubling you My Lady" she said, in her warm Derbyshire brogue "- it ain't nothing a little sustenance and companionship can't fix."

"It's very good of you to say so, Mary" she replied, feeling maudlin, "- nevertheless, I fear that there is no solution to my present predicament. The heart is like a tar-pit at times, you can fall into it and struggle to ever get out, no matter how much it burns you."

"Well I'm not so sure about that, My Lady" Mary said, refusing, like all of the kindest people, to indulge her too much in her ill mood. "I think there's always comfort to be sought if you're mindful and know yourself well."

At first this statement had little effect upon Charlotte's ill humour, but it slowly started to make some impact, working its way into her thoughts, and providing some comfort.

Within only a short space of time at least a few of Charlotte's troubles were banished. There was a sudden swell of activity, and the sounds of sudden activity drew Charlotte out of her room, curiosity overcoming her miseries.  She looked on in surprise as servants and footmen scurried towards the front of the house to prepare a formal reception.

Like Charlotte, many of the guests also followed the procession of agitated servants, curious as to what had stirred it into action. Charlotte found herself almost running towards the door, caught up in the tide, trying to catch what people were feverishly whispering at each other by way of explanation. And then she heard it, just two words, the syllables that had been haunting her dreams.

"... Don Diego has arrived!"

She could not make out who had said it, but she was immediately grateful to them. The knowledge brought her a fresh burst of joy for just a few moments, but also a nervousness, and a little worry that things might not go quite as she had hoped. So much had been invested in this moment, so much of herself, heart and mind and soul, and yet it was entirely possible that, from the Don's perspective, she was no more than a passing fancy. Her experience of the previous night had not aided her faith in the behaviour of gentlemen.

The main doors opened, no more forcefully than usual, but with a force to Charlotte's eye that seemed to slam them wide. Footmen stood to attention, and the Argentine strode in, as gloriously attired as ever, confident and forthright.

"Don Diego Sanchez-Zapata, Count of San Pedro" boomed the voice of the butler, hurriedly announcing the Don to all and sundry.

Most had never previously made his acquaintance, and did not even bother to disguise their wonder at the arrival of this exotic novelty. He looked splendid in his red and gold uniform, with a proud blue sash that seemed to give him a warrior air, invincible and dominant.

Charlotte was unsure whether it was her foreknowledge of his incredible dancing skills, but she felt that he walked with a stronger motion compared to Englishmen, bolder, at a different pace.

She was as compelled, instantly drawn to him, on seeing him again, as she had been when they had first made each other's acquaintance, barely a fortnight ago.

"Don Diego!" boomed Lady Derbyshire, hurrying down the stairs to greet her latest guest "- we had feared you might not be able to attend! It is surely our great pleasure and privilege to host you!"

"Truly, my Lady" he replied, with all of the same dusky promise he seemed to bring to all of his interactions "-the pleasure is entirely mine. I only regret that I could not be present at the wedding ceremony, I have already heard that it was a wonderful occasion, only my business in London detained me longer than I had hoped."

"We are extremely grateful for your presence, Don Diego, there is no need for you to trouble yourself with apologies on our account."

"My Lady is as courteous as ever" he said, stooping to kiss his host's hand.

Charlotte felt frozen in place, her eyes fixed on him, desperately willing him to look up and meet her gaze, but she was partially concealed behind a rank of staff, tangled in the cluster of curious guests, and could not bring herself to push forward desperately and impolitely, despite her intense longing to do so.

In the end, she regretfully stepped back again, and left the Don and his servants to get on with the process of moving in, in peace.

Before she left however, she could not help but notice a woman in Don Diego's company, not dressed in livery and carrying luggage like his servants, but instead clad in a sumptuous red and gold dress that she presumed was the costume of a Spanish or Argentine noblewoman.

She had thick dark hair and pale caramel coloured skin, as one would expect of a woman of her climate and culture, and pillowed red lips that seemed, even to Charlotte's naïve eye, to be full of what many men would consider to be promise.

Many of the men present, even the servants, threw her a few longing glances, responding instinctively to the sense of lust and fantasy that she had ushered into Amfield House.

It was troubling, and gave Charlotte a small sense of dread that she felt she should address at once. Her curiosity was raised, and, after the events of the previous evening, she did not like feeling any sense of uncertainty.

"Mother" she asked Lady Derbyshire once the party of new arrivals had passed on up the stairs "Do you happen to know who that young woman in Don Diego's company is?"

Lady Derbyshire's eyes immediately narrowed in suspicion. She had seen her daughter dance with the handsome Argentine at the last ball at Amfield, just a few short weeks ago, and had more than enough intuition to have her suspicions aroused by this new enquiry.

"Why yes, as it happens, I do" she said.

"She is Senora Anna-Maria Hernandez, a recent widow who has come into Don Diego's wardship, due to distant family ties and…" Lady Derbyshire paused to consider the wording of her next sentence "- it is whispered, also his former fiancée. Whether or not there is any, closeness, shall we say, between them is anyone's guess."

On this ominous note, she left Charlotte to fuss and contemplate the situation alone.

# Chapter Eight

The Don was not seen again for the early part of that day, but Charlotte was unable to take her mind off him for even a second. In her defence, even had she been able to avoid thinking of him, none of the guests would allow her to, as they constantly reminded her by whispering, over tea and cakes, a range of mostly unlikely rumours about the Argentine, and the woman who most there presumed to be his mistress.

"Well I, for one, consider it most improper of him to have arrived with that fallen woman in tow." Lady Frome spoke piously, but with a hint of enjoyment all the same. "Foreigner or no, one does not fly in the face of the hospitality of one's hosts so flagrantly, would you not agree, Herbert?" she prodded her husband, who seemed to be drifting off to sleep in his chair.

"Hmm?" he exclaimed, like a bear at the end of its winter's hibernation "oh yes, yes, absolutely." Charlotte had long suspected that he had mastered the art of answering Lady Frome's questions without ever having to actually listen to what she had said at all.

"It may very well be usual in South America to drag hussies along to wedding parties, but in Derbyshire it is quite out of the question. Why I don't believe even a Frenchman would stoop so low."

"I've heard…" said another woman, Lady Gillforth, a soft-spoken old countess from Berkshire "- that the Don and this Hernandez woman were once engaged, back in their own country, but that he had to break it off after he found her carousing with another gentleman in the Don's very own bedchamber!"

"Thin walls in the Tropics" piped up her husband, the Marquess of Gillforth, from behind his enormous moustache. He was a large man in every conceivable sense, and had no qualms about expressing his opinions bluntly and with frequency. "No sense of propriety at all. Heat brings out unseemly passions. Un-Christian climate too. None of it should surprise anyone. They're all bad to the bone."

"I would not be quite so quick to make so general a judgement, My Lord." Charlotte could not help herself but reply immediately.

The red-faced look of disgust she got in return from the Marquess made her regret her interjection straight away. Nonetheless, she continued gamely, unwilling to leave her comment incomplete.

"The Latin races have, by my estimation, a strong sense of virtue and honour which I myself witnessed in the company of the Don when last he was at Amfield."

"I shall have to make a judgement of the chap's character for myself." Gillforth replied, clearly annoyed at the impudence of this girl, who nevertheless, as the daughter of his hosts, could not be dismissed out of hand.

"But by my reckoning, dagos and their mistresses can all rot". Charlotte, feeling herself to be the only one present scandalized by such a sweeping opinion, made her excuses and went to find another conversation.

She could not escape either the shadow of the Don, or Hemsbridge. They were both there all the time, either by dint of their physical presence, or the gossip of others, prompting her to think unpleasant, unhelpful, miserable and self-doubting thoughts.

The Englishman, with whom she had only yesterday cavorted in the gardens, seemed to be avoiding her in the main, skirting around the edges of her conversations and avoiding eye contact wherever possible. The Argentine, on the other hand, was everywhere, charming everyone with his energy and passion, and yet, at the same time, the subject of so many salacious rumours that it was almost too much to bear.

At last, evening came, and with it the opportunity for more dancing as the string quartet tuned up their instruments and more bowls of punch were brought to fuel the young ladies and gentlemen in their endeavours. It was not quite a ball, but it was certainly a large gathering, as most guests would not depart for another day at least.

Charlotte retired to her room to change into a dress more suited to an evening function like this. A difficult choice, as she felt that she needed to be more formal than normal, but not quite so formal as for an actual ball.

With Mary's help she selected a dress that she knew was one of her finest, a gold trimmed burgundy muslin frock with lightly puffed small sleeves that barely sat on her shoulders and a fashionably low back which she knew would immediately attract the attention of the gentlemen present. It gave away just enough, revealing enough creamy white skin, without being inappropriate for her age, to be enticing in just the right way.

She was silent, too anxious to speak much to her domestic confidante, who simply smiled encouragingly as she carried out her duties, letting Charlotte simmer in her own thoughts. She allowed her mind to wander, towards the possibilities that the evening entailed, towards dashing Argentine Counts and piercing Marquess' eyes, to the kiss she had shared with her Don, not so very long ago, in this very house, and the power that it had seemed to have over her. Oh for a repeat of those feelings, a re-run of that delicious shivering encounter they'd had on the stairs.

Regarding herself full length in the mirror, she saw herself for the first time from the perspective of a gentleman, and was pleased. She was, she decided, pretty after all - Blanche did not have an exclusive monopoly on male attention, she would have her own great love affair and light up all of the great houses of England with her beauty and grace. All she needed now, was an appropriate suitor. Once in the salon itself however, Charlotte felt quite inhibited by the entire situation.

She could not, as a lady, make any advances of her own, of course, but she did have some say over who she graced with her attention, who she made eye contact with and the manner of her attentions and bearing to try and entice the man of her choosing to her. The problem was who?

She was approached briefly, despite making no advances of any sort, by young William Banbury, her temporary partner from the other evening (was it only last night? It felt like a lifetime ago). Witnessing him gulp down a stiff measure of punch for confidence, there was nothing she could do to prevent him from coming over:

"You look as radiant as ever, Lady Charlotte" he said, like a man who had been thinking about his words a little too much.

"Why thank you, Mr. Banbury" she replied coyly "- you are most kind."

"I would be deeply honoured if you would consider joining me in this next dance." Charlotte turned and looked Banbury directly in the eye. He was a pleasant fellow and she bore him no ill will, and yet he stirred no passion in her. Next to the other men vying for attention in her mind and exercising the interest of her very soul, she could not bring herself to deceive the poor fellow any further.

"I am most flattered by your attentions sir" she said, considering her words very carefully and doing everything she could to avoid spite "However, I am afraid, that, on this occasion, I am compelled to refuse. I had a most unpleasant attack of the vapours earlier today, and I am still feeling not quite up to the mark. I think that I will begin the evening quietly."

It was, of course, all a lie, but a white lie with which she hoped not to wound her childhood friend too deeply. It seemed to have the desired effect, as he fixed her with a look of sympathy rather than hurt pride.

"I am deeply sorry to hear so, My Lady" he said "-please, accept my consolations." Charlotte was relieved to watch him walk off with his confidence intact.

Unfortunately, Charlotte's story was soon to be rather undermined. For mere minutes later, Don Diego made his appearance, unaccompanied, to the small disappointment of many of the gentlemen present, who had hoped, it was obvious, to make the acquaintance of Senora Hernandez.

As far as the ladies were concerned however, the sight of the Don was more than enough. He radiated an inner fire, moving with an effervescent boldness that drew all eyes towards him. He seemed to have styled his hair in a new fashion, more fitting with English society and perhaps learned in London.

Otherwise however, his appearance matched his nationality perfectly. His skin was a rich tan colour, almost dun in the parlance of the English countryside, yet unlike a ploughman lashed by the elements, his darkness had a shimmering beauty to it, perfectly complemented by his dark eyes.

He had high cheekbones creating a shapely, angular face, smooth to the touch but with hints of rougher, harder qualities no doubt honed in the rough grasslands of his homeland.

There was an ageless quality to him, for though he was younger than the beginnings of lines on his face suggested, he had an air of experience and surety about him, finely balanced by his vivacious energy.

Charlotte knew, straight away, that she had been right to push aside the rather inappropriate advances of Hemsbridge in favour of this man. She trembled with excitement and ardently hoped that he would remember their previous encounter.

Within moments, she had an answer to all of the questions, which had assailed her mind and heart since that fateful evening, when she had last had the chance to speak to him.

All that had been on her mind since that time was the same, recurring dilemma - is he thinking of me as I am of him? Does passion stir in his soul at the thought of my body and presence as mine does at the idea of his? And will that kiss on the stairs prove to be more than a passing moment of attraction, and blossom into anything more profound?

The letter that she had obsessed over, the sleepless nights that she had spent fidgeting into oblivion, tossing and turning, all came apart and melted away into the irrelevant past as he walked towards her. He had exchanged some pleasantries with her parents and then with a few of the other assembled dignitaries, who were grouped in conversational clusters around the edge of the room (including, to Charlotte's amusement, the disapproving Lord Gillforth), and then made directly for her.

"Lady Charlotte" he said, in a voice that sliced like a rapier straight to her heart, claiming it as the Argentine's own in an instant. "- it brings me great joy to see you again."

"It is very generous of your Lordship to have come" she said, using every ounce of energy that she possessed to contain her desire to squeal in delight and wrap her arms around his neck at once.

Custom, position, and the demands of formal politeness could often be a bore at best, as far as Charlotte was concerned, but at times like this they were tyrannical. It was impossible to express anything of the contents of either head or heart in this rigid, customary idiom.

"I trust you find Amfield once again to your liking?"

"Truly there is no finer house in all of England, save perhaps, the palaces of the king himself. My own newly acquired estate, in Buckinghamshire, pales in comparison to this great place."

"Modesty compels me to object, sir" she said, prompting a genuine and spontaneous laugh from the Don. That laugh was all the prompting Charlotte needed to have her heart set racing ahead, pounding out an insistent rhythm. Their rapport appeared to have continued, "- although I suppose having grown up here am I little over-used to it."

"Then you shall have to visit me some time, at my aforementioned residence" he said, entirely lacking the coyness and steady manner of an Englishman, surrendering himself to earnest, soulful expressions.

"I am planning to host a party there at some point, to mark my renaming of it. It is to be called Rosario Mansions, in honour of my favourite estate, my lost home."

"My sincerest condolences, my Lord" Charlotte replied softly. She had heard about the Don's being, in his native Argentina, stripped of his title by the revolutionary government that had taken charge of Argentina, in place of the Spanish Crown. That government had declared all noble titles void in Argentina, even though the Spanish still recognised the Argentine nobility.

It was a difficult and complex affair that had led to Diego's exile here in his second-favourite land.

She knew that she was on unstable ground discussing this. "- it is a terrible tragedy that has befallen your house."

He stared, pained, into the middle distance for a moment, obviously recalling memories of places he might never visit again, might have lost forever.

Charlotte was overwhelmed with a desire to comfort him, to soothe the pain he expressed so fluently with only his eyes.

"I will not deny the truth of what you have said. It pains me greatly that I may never see my homeland again. Yet here, I have a new home, and I am determined to make the most of that. For what is life, if not a constant series of tests and adversities? To feel pain is to feel a necessary component of one's own humanity."

"A most worthy sentiment, my Lord."

"I should hope so. And now, my Lady Charlotte, I would be deeply honoured, and feel a small sense of relief from the agony in my heart, if you would join me in a dance."

Charlotte's entire being seemed to lift upwards at these words.

She was compelled to stand almost upon the points of her toes, and had to bite her tongue to stop herself from leaping for joy into the air. Inwardly, she swelled and pulsed for him, her heart feeling like it might burst from the strain.

'I think that would be most fitting, My Lord, and a great pleasure to me.'

"Wonderful." Immediately, without bothering to take her hand and walk her to the centre of the room, and almost completely ignoring the rather sedate music of the traditional country dance being played by the musicians, the Argentine exile instead seized her firmly and pulled her in for the commencement of one of his passionate Latin dances, moving in time to the music that only he could hear, in his imagination.

They started, as befitted this first encounter, and as made some concession to the pace of the string quartet, slowly. With practised ease, Don Diego brought his hand to the small of Charlotte's back, pulling her towards him. Charlotte glanced over at her mother, half-expecting Lady Derbyshire to be shaking her head in disapproval, and moving to prevent the dance from going ahead. Instead, as their eyes met, she could discern a small nod from the older woman, and an approving raise of the eyebrow.

Charlotte could not help but raise a smile at this tiny moment of consent, and hope that those looking on at the unorthodox manner of her dancing would not think ill of either her or the Don for it. As other couples came to join them on the dance floor, albeit proceeding with the more traditional English country dance, some of the attention, which Charlotte had feared would be negative, started to subside.

With less space, and a greater expectation of co-ordination between the various couples, the Don lapsed instinctively into something akin to, but not the same as, the dance that the others were performing, getting into line with the various English gentlemen around him, many of whom had been casting wary glances at the serpentine hips and rapid feet of the Argentine.

The music, and their bodily proximity, was all the while bringing Charlotte closer and closer to feelings of warmth and pleasure. She loved the feeling of his strong arms about her, of his lean waist pressed close to hers, of their twirling and swirling motions like eddies in a still pool of water. Arousal and hope were intertwined in their arms.

It was at this moment, though, that Charlotte made eye contact with Hemsbridge.

She had not seen him in the room earlier, and had presumed that he was otherwise engaged for the evening, or else had headed back to Somerset after the disappointment of the previous night. Now however he was standing alone, giving off a dark, brooding air, although immaculately presented in a bottle green dress coat, of a colour close to his eyes, his shock of red-brown hair drawing her eye to his end of the room.

Charlotte almost gasped into Don Diego's ear. What were his thoughts at this moment? She could not tell, but even at a distance his eyes betrayed a scalding resentment, a feeling of envy and possessiveness towards her, and of bitterness towards the Argentine, who was now very much the toast of the ball. Then suddenly, wolf-like, he was on the move, stalking towards them. Leaving the corner in which he had been standing alone, sipping at punch and throwing out glares, he advanced, pushing past several couples on his way forward.

Charlotte was aware that Don Diego had no knowledge of her acquaintance with the fellow, indeed, it was likely that Don Diego had no idea even of who he was. She fiercely dreaded the idea of the two coming to some sort of confrontation, of Hemsbridge spilling out some dark truth from the night before, or her honour being brought into question by either man.

Hemsbridge still held some modicum of attraction for her, but her feelings were deeply confused by his aggressive actions of the night before, and Don Diego was the man that she had dreamed of now for weeks. That this blissful communion might be disrupted by an interjection over an ill-advised fumble the previous evening chilled her to the bone.

"If I might interject for a moment." Hemsbridge spoke confidently. The Don, impassive, continued his latest encircling movement with an easy flourish, and turned to face the intruder.

"Yes, my good man?" he said, in a voice that aimed at innocent enquiry, but revealed his displeasure at the interruption.

"I should like to dance with the young lady, if that would be acceptable to you, sir." There was a boldness to the Englishman's speech that caused both Charlotte and Diego to stop in their tracks and look directly at him.

They paused and pondered, taking a few steps to the left to take them out of the paths of other couples. Charlotte could barely believe the impudence of the man, and yet his confidence was also a little alluring. He could not possibly know the history between the two before him, or what mighty elemental forces moved inside her, driven by her intense attraction to the Don.

He was merely another gentleman at a ball, asking a lady to dance with him, at least as far as he, or any of the onlookers were concerned. Charlotte glanced past his shoulder to look for her mother, only to find that Lord and Lady Derbyshire were distracted, talking to the Bishop and partaking of a glass of wine.

"I trust you shall dance with my Lady Charlotte with both capability and honour, although I must say that I find your timing, and manner of asking, rather impertinent." Don Diego said, at last breaking the tension. "Now if you'll excuse me, there is a little personal business which must draw me away from the room for a little time."

He promptly took his leave, laying a kiss on Charlotte's hand, bowing briskly to her mother and father, and then deserting the ballroom as suddenly and impulsively as he had entered.

Hemsbridge did not waste any time in taking her whole body firmly in his grasp and commencing to dance.

"Your Don Diego is quite the dancer, my Lady." Hemsbridge's voice was low, almost sultry, close to her ear. "Evidently, all of the clichés spoken of his race have some element of truth to them. Tell me, do you find him attractive?"

"Sir!" Charlotte could not help but exclaim in reply. "I think that question to be entirely impertinent and inappropriate - I will not answer it!"

"I shall take that for a yes, then" he smiled, wryly. "I do not think you find yourself alone in pursuit of the Argentine's affections. Nor indeed alone in receiving them."

She instinctively dug her fingers into his back in response to this. He interpreted the gesture as one of arousal, and interest in his attentions, and pulled her closer to him, as he had the previous night.

This was not however, what she had meant to communicate, and she found herself pulling away slightly, concerned at the impetuousness of this young Marquess.

"I cannot possibly imagine what that is supposed to mean." She spoke firmly, unhappy with the entire conversation. "Don Diego is a Count of Buenos Aires province, and a long-cherished acquaintance of my family, I cannot understand why you, and for that matter, many of the others here, insist upon bringing his morality into question."

"I shall answer that question…" continued Hemsbridge, looking darkly into the middle distance.

Despite her horror at his conduct, Charlotte did feel a momentary touch of attraction towards him in that instant. Their proximity created a shadow that brought out the fine curvature of his jaw, and she was, for just a second, teetering on the brink of the same passions that had moved her, initially, in the Italian garden, "- with a single image, that of this Anna-Maria woman, who appears to be entirely without any notion of title or breeding, even for an Argentine or Spaniard. What, pray, have you surmised as being her place and purpose in all of this?"

He looked at her now, fixing her in the gaze of his big, green eyes, a green as lush as a fresh-cut pasture.

"I am told…" Charlotte made to respond, but she could not possibly fathom it. It was all too horrible, the thought of Don Diego having some mistress out of wedlock whom he carried around with him to use for unspeakable, wanton purposes.

She did not wish to believe that he could possibly indulge himself in such a manner, and yet she could find in her head no counter-argument robust enough to dismiss the theory entirely.

It was possible, she had to concede to herself, that if he was once engaged to that woman, then perhaps she was still his mistress, his lover, his – she could hardly bear even to think the word, let alone pronounce it - his whore.

A tear formed in the corner of her eye but she would not allow Hemsbridge the satisfaction of watching it trickle down her face.

"... and what of this 'personal business' to which he is now so urgently attending?"

"Oh stop it sir!" she hissed, just managing to contain her public exclamation so that only he could hear. "Your endless questions bring me nothing but enervation! And I find the salacious topic of your conversation a highly improper one for conversing with a well-bred young lady! Thank you for the dance."

Charlotte untangled herself from the Marquess' grip and hurriedly, hoping she went unnoticed, but too caught up in the racing thoughts of that moment to really tell, dashed out of the ballroom to find shelter and, she prayed, the Don.

# Chapter Nine

Charlotte cried. She had hoped that she would not, that she would be able to contain any outbursts of feeling and instead consider her position in a sober and rational manner, but it had proven impossible. The one shining silver tear, which Hemsbridge's words had brought suddenly to life, now multiplied into a torrent of weeping, the tears streaming down her face. She sobbed and sobbed, gasping in air dramatically, grateful that no-one had seen her. Listlessly, she made her way through the corridors of Amfield House, until she found her way into the library. It was deserted, as she had suspected it would be, and suitably out of the way to allow her to rid herself of these emotional ructions in peace.

It was, she was forced once again to concede, entirely possible that Hemsbridge was right in the things that he had said about Don Diego.

She had not, of course, had the opportunity to ask Don Diego about his relationship with this Hernandez woman, about why she was here and what had detained him from joining the rest of the party for so long, both at its commencement and then during the day. It filled her with sadness to consider the possibility of the two of them cavorting in each other's arms, of Diego, her Diego, who she had convinced herself, in her girlish inexperience, that she loved, skulking off to make love to another woman. A woman from his own culture and with whom he had pursued an affair in the past. Such a situation would cast her merely as a pleasant distraction, exotic for her Englishness, but perhaps inadequate next to this well-seasoned Spanish beauty.

And then there was Hemsbridge. There was no denying that he was a flawed character, as his behaviour both the other evening in the gardens, and just now upon the dancefloor, had very much demonstrated. But he was still the same devilishly handsome young Marquess she had set her eye upon the first day of the wedding celebrations, in the church, and she could not help but feel a slight trembling beneath her petticoats every time she saw him, or pictured him in her mind's eye, or imagined him kissing her and holding her close to him once again. She was not at all sure whether she liked that trembling, and the little shiver that went through her when she thought of what he had done.

Perhaps, if he was right and Don Diego's morals were suspect, at least by the standards of the provincial English nobility, then perhaps a man like him, closer to her own class and type, would be a more appropriate match.

She considered the prospect of weening herself off her intense Latin fantasies in favour of the young lord from Somerset, but try as she might, she could not feel much joy at the idea.

It was at this moment that she was interrupted in her contemplations by the sound of the door. Expecting that it was either a servant come to clear away any lingering detritus, or worse, a couple who were escaping away from the prying eyes of the chaperones, she sat up abruptly, worried that she was to be disturbed and then interrogated on why she was alone, away from the party, and what the source of the tears running down her face might be.

This was all too much to face and she considered hiding behind one of the bookshelves, or even making a dash for the windowed doors to the terrace and setting off into the grounds, to find her way back to the party, or maybe even her bedchamber, via the servants' entrance. But when she looked up, all of this anxiety was dispelled. She was overwhelmed by a feeling of hopeful surprise, and her entire life seemed at once to be set upon the right course. For entering the library, without knocking or seemingly expecting to find it occupied, was Don Diego Sanchez-Zapata, Count of San Pedro, the shadow hanging over all her dreams.

"My Lady" he exclaimed, his voice sounding surprised for the first time in their brief acquaintance. He usually had such an air of easy composure about him, as if interactions for him were an almost spiritual experience, rather than a complex challenge. This air soon returned to his voice and bearing. "- I had not expected to find you in here…"

"I suppose it would be rather strange if you had, my Lord" she replied, wishing that her tears would somehow find a way of working their way back into her eyes. They would not, of course, they sat there glistening, betraying her feelings, "- the library is not considered a conventional venue for social occasions such as this." He laughed a little at her remark.

"No indeed, I suppose it is not" he said, moving towards her as confidently and purposefully as ever. "I had hoped to come here to find some quiet refuge, but I see that you have, as you say, beaten me to it?" he sat beside her on the long, leather-bound chaise, looking imploringly into her still tearful eyes. "My Lady Charlotte, you speak, as you English so often do, in polite and good-humoured tones, yet I can see from your face that this does not match the feelings in your heart."

He took her soft, milky white hands in his, pressing his toughened palms against her fingers. She sighed heavily, letting out this impenetrable blend of pain, compassion and longing. Social convention dictated that she should not, yet she felt safe enough to pour out her feelings to this man.

"You have quite found me out of course" she said, suppressing a sob, accepting his offer of a silk handkerchief. It smelled fragrant, almost spicy, in a way that was unfamiliar to her, but so distinctly part of him. "I came here because…" what could she say?

She could not let out the dilemmas that moved her to him, because he was at their heart! Enough of the advice generally given to young ladies had penetrated her conscious mind that she knew not to simply spill out her feelings, but it was difficult to hold them in.

"You came, I expect, because you feel a conflict in your heart, a division within your soul" he looked at her firmly, warmly, seductively. "I sense it, Lady Charlotte, in your bearing, and it is a most difficult burden. I myself, feel it also. Sometimes, what we must do is simply to surrender ourselves to the glory, the beauty of the moment, allow ourselves to be lost in another's contemplation." He pronounced this sentiment in a quiet, sensuous voice, which seemed to brush like velvet over her skin.

They leant towards each other, seemingly drawn, like iron to a magnet, helplessly to each other, and before either had any time to contemplate their actions he was kissing her, placing gentle, yet passionate kisses all over her face, drifting delicate touches across her lips, tasting her skin. She sighed, delighted by the sensations, lifting her arms to encircle his neck and returning his kisses with enthusiasm, if no great experience

Charlotte felt flushed, breathless, her rapid heartbeat pulsating, shaking her with the intensity of her feelings in response to this consummation of her desires, this delivery into reality of the stuff of her imagination.  All of the fears and dilemmas of the last few hours were promptly banished by an ecstatic rush of delight, and the delicious pleasure of the physical sensations of his touch. It was a marvellous thing to have communicated to her, in this impulsive, physical manner, that she was not alone in her feelings.

Sensation ran all over her body, the surprise of new feelings making her momentarily recoil at his touch only to plunge herself more deeply towards him, seeking to be as close as she possibly could, as they kissed and kissed and held each other close.

Unlike Hemsbridge the previous evening, the Don was not forceful, aggressive or overly insistent in his motions. He used his lips and tongue with great care and consideration, allowing her at times to lead and dictate the pace of their kisses, at others firmly assuming command.

His hands were light and subtle in their movements, soft enough to not feel demanding or grasping, but firm enough to send shivers all through her as he slid his hands over her breasts and slid them down her sides to her waist, pressing himself against her. Her nipples tingled in response, and her mouth opened more to his kisses as her body arched against him, seeking more of his touch.

Then, without warning, he pulled away, placing one final, tender kiss on her forehead before rising to his feet.

"I am sorry, my Lady" he said, smoothing his fine clothing back down, as if forcing himself back to his calm and imposing appearance after the impetuous passions of a few moments ago. "I must return to my private affairs. You arouse great feelings in me, but I feel that at this stage, for me to consummate those fully would be a violation of you and of your family's honour. I am not sorry that I have kissed you, for truly, you are a delight, but I am sorry that I have accosted you in such an ungentlemanly fashion as this." He bowed, kissing her hand, and went to leave the room.

As he turned to go Charlotte could not quite contain her sadness. She longed for him, yearned for him, throbbed for him right from the top of her head to the most sensitive parts beneath her frock, between her legs.

A shiver of desire ran up and down the insides of her thighs and into her belly, making it quiver in expectation. She could not just let him leave her like this.

"Wait, my Lord!" she exclaimed, just as he was approaching the door.

"My room is the third left in the west wing, of the floor above." He turned to face her, his face betraying surprise at her sudden boldness. "If, that is, you feel the need for any human company, and further conversation, during the night."

"You are most generous, miss" he said, bowing solemnly, as she presumed was customary in his culture. "However, as delightful as I have found your company, I feel I must respect the hospitality of your house, and the honour of your good family. I would not want my actions misinterpreted. We will speak further, on the morrow."

With an extravagant flourish of his hand, he was off, about whatever business it was that so distracted him. Charlotte stood for a moment, not a little disappointed, but still quivering with excitement at the possibility of seeing more of this remarkable man.

She could not possibly face re-joining the party. She thought for a while, settled in the security of the library, about doing so, and she even stepped out into the corridors of Amfield House, intending to do so, but finally decided against it. She could not face Hemsbridge, or dispel the thought of Don Diego, and the kisses that had so branded her skin with the heat of their passion that she felt the warmth still, so instead she found her way quietly to her room, and sat by her bed, too stimulated to sleep.

She tried reading a novel that she had been picking her way through recently, but found that she could not concentrate for long enough to absorb more than a few sentences at a time, and that all that any of the words spelled out was *Don Diego, Don Diego.* She tried writing in her diary, but found that her words were not at all adequate to express this jubilant feeling. She was full of new energy and vitality, and found herself without a moment's thought, or any lingering trace of inhibition, dancing and leaping around her room as if it were the most normal and natural thing in the world, with merry tunes running through her head.

Finally, exhausted but still consumed with happiness, she simply lay on top of her bed outside the sheets, still wearing her full evening gown, surrounded by the same room that had been hers since childhood but feeling herself sliding rapidly into the mind and skin of a full-grown woman. And then at last, just as sleep seemed finally to be creeping up on her, there was a gentle knocking at her door.

"Who is it?" she said, sitting up on the bed and trying to compose herself. She assumed that it must be a servant, come to bring her a fresh chamber pot, or her maid come to help her ready for bed, or else a lost guest who'd taken a few too many measures of punch, staggering back to their room. She did not dare allow herself to believe that it could be the source of her happiness, the bringer of her delights.

"Come in" she said after receiving no reply. She fidgeted to put her dress to rights, only then noticing the state of disarray that had resulted from her leaping about, and collapsing onto the bed with no thought for her appearance.

She looked away trying to remain casual, but there was no mistaking that the door was creaking open to reveal Don Diego, still attired in his evening wear and beaming a great smile at her.

He closed the door carefully, and turned towards her. "Forgive my intrusion" he said, striding confidently towards her, where she sat on the bed, " – but I could not bear to be parted from you for any longer, Lady Charlotte." She sprang up and walked into his arms and his kiss, with the same sense of inevitability and desire that had brought them together in the library. Surrounded by his arms simply seemed the right place to be.

She gave herself up to the sensation of his fervent passion, accepting his powerful embrace, letting her lips part and allowing his tongue to explore, to meet and tangle with hers. These were new sensations, confusing and delightful at once. Whilst the actions were the same, somehow the sensations that they created in her were completely different from those that she had felt with Hemsbridge.  She would puzzle over that conundrum later – for now she allowed herself to simply delight in his touch.

His kisses aroused her, made her breath come short and her breasts feel hot and swollen, her nipples sensitive and aching where they rubbed against the edge of her corset. His hands held her to him, and slid over her body, tracing her shape from the nape of her neck to her waist, leaving tingling in their wake.

He was strong, and his smell was exciting – not like any person or thing that she knew, exotic and compelling, exciting all by itself.  It wove around her, intoxicating.

The feeling of her breasts crushed against his hard muscled chest excited her more, and she brought her hands up, to slide up his chest, and settle around his neck.  The sensations were so strong that her knees felt weak, and she clung to him as they became entirely overwhelming, so powerful in fact that she entirely forgot where she was, that this was the room and the house that she had grown up in.

He lifted her, easily, as if she weighed nothing, and carried her to the bed, kissing her still. He laid her down gently, and joined her on the bed, his kisses never pausing, his body partly over hers, never forceful, passionate but considerate in the manner of his performance. He transported her with his skilled hands and agile mouth, away from Amfield, away from Derbyshire, away even from rigid English upper-class society altogether, across the seas to Argentina.

She felt the warmth of his country, the music and poetry, the life so much less hindered by formality and discipline, and it pleased her more profoundly than she had ever been pleased before.

"Oh, Don Diego…" she panted his name, feeling the heat of their passion rising from her breasts, as they rose and fell against his hard chest with the uneven pattern of her aroused breathing. She thought, with a tiny, amused portion of her brain, that now she understood what all those horrid novels meant when they spoke of women with 'heaving bosoms'.

"I do not wish to alarm you…" he said, kissing her neck and bringing out of her a feverish burst of energy, making her arch up towards his kisses.

"No, no…" was all she could say in response, and without even knowing what she was doing she pulled him tighter to her, her hands, desperate to touch him, scratching and pawing at his coat like a cat. As one they surrendered to passion and sensation, indulging desire with endless kisses, with the taste of each other's lips and skin.

She gave in to his hands and fingers, working their way into her petticoats and pressing firmly against her most precious and vital folds of skin. For a moment she stiffened, her mind going back to Hemsbridge, and the previous evening, but only for a moment. His touch was firm, yet delicate and careful, skilled and considerate. It was an utterly different, and wholly pleasant, experience.

His kisses trailed down her neck, finding her nipples through the thin fabric of the top of her gown, and his fingers worked to build the sensations of pleasure to a new intensity, working intricate patterns with an incredible sensuality on her most intimate flesh, drawing forth a heat and wetness that she had not expected of these new passions. She found that she craved more and more of his touch, that, without understanding why, she wanted him to do as Hemsbridge had and more, to drive his fingers inside her, into that most secret place.

Every part of her seemed to stand on end, every inch of her skin craved his touch, and his breath as it caressed her was pleasure and torture at once. Her mind was bursting with feelings she could not ever hope to express in mere words. Instead she gasped and closed her eyes, throwing her head back, giving herself to him, willing him to continue for as long as he liked to please her more.

Gently, he slid the sleeves of her dress from her shoulders, pulling the bodice down to free her nipples to his touch. She gasped as the cool air touched the heated points, then gasped again as his warm tongue caressed them, sending sensations shooting to her core with every brush of his mouth on her skin. He drew one hard point into his mouth and suckled it, alternately licking, and catching it gently with his teeth, until she cried out at the pleasure, helplessly arching her hips up towards him.

"Oh,… Oh…. Please…" her words were ragged, and she realised that she did not know what she was asking him to do, just that she needed something more. In response, he turned his attentions to her other breast, and, as she arched hard in response, he slid his finger inside her, slowly at first, then beginning to move it, in and out, in time with his kisses at her breast. She sighed in pleasure, amazed at how delicious it felt, wanting more, working her hips in time with his hand, somehow just instinctively knowing what to do.

After a short time, she felt the sensations building strongly, and realised that there must be more, that she wanted more, somehow. He had brought a second finger to play, and as she begged him again, he laughed gently. 'Patience my darling – I am making sure that you will have the most pleasure possible.'

Shifting slightly, he pulled her skirts up, to pool around her waist, a rich gold and burgundy tangle on the bedcovers, and slid, trailing kisses as he went, down her body. She felt the pressure of his hard manhood against her leg as he moved, and wondered when she would touch him.

That train of thought was rapidly derailed, as he pushed the clothing aside, expertly opening the slit in her drawers further, and brought his mouth to her most intimate parts. She was shocked, and then lost all capacity for thought, as his skilful tongue stroked her, finding the most sensitive spot, and began to work in time with the fingers that he moved within her. Instantly, the build of pleasure escalated, and she cried out his name, squirming and writhing with the sensations that he raised in her body.

Charlotte felt desperate, felt as if there was something so close, that she wanted, but did not know how to reach it. She slid her fingers into his hair, clasping him to her, arching her hips to his touch, gasping and crying out her need. He redoubled his efforts and then, without warning, she felt her world explode, as a wave of pleasure rocked through her, pulling a little scream from her throat and a spasming crescendo of movement from her body.

"Oh.... I had no idea..." she whispered, drifting back from the whirlwind of pleasure. She realised that, whilst she had been oblivious the last few minutes, he had somehow dextrously undone his falls, easing the no doubt severe pressure on his arousal. His manhood jutted proudly, and she reached a tentative hand to touch him, delighted when he drew a sharp breath at her touch, and his eyes darkened with a deeper desire and passion.

The skin that she touched was warm, velvety, and the hardness beneath it shocking in its strength. She moved her hand, watching his reactions, pleased to see how much pleasure it gave him.

He leant to kiss her again, drifting kisses across her lips and face, across her neck and in a trail down the silken skin of her breasts, to suckle and lick again at her nipples, until they were both breathing hard, and her hips were moving uncontrollably in response.

"Please, Diego, please, I want more, please…." He stilled at her words, lifting his head to look into her eyes.

"Charlotte, my darling, are you sure?  I should not, we should not…."

"Shhh, I am sure, so very sure, love me my Don, please…"

At those words a low groan escaped him and he shifted position and in a smooth moment had pulled her skirts and drawers even further apart, exposing her to his gaze. She did not mind that she was exposed – it seemed so right, so much a part of the fact that she simply wanted, wanted to be his, wanted to feel him inside her, wanted more, more of the pleasure that he could give her.

Then she saw his face change, as his desire for her overcame all remaining restraint, and all the passionate sensuality of Argentina and his Latin race came to the fore. He moved over her, and she welcomed him with her arms, arching her hips up to meet him, and crying out with pleasure, and the sharp little pain, as he entered her with a groan and a single thrust. She shuddered, she had not expected the pain, but it was not so intense, and fading rapidly.

Sheathed deep within her, he paused a moment, kissing her gently, until he felt her relax a little, becoming used to the feeling of being filled.

Then he began to move, gently at first, then faster, as Charlotte responded, beginning to move with him, to meet his thrusts with raised hips and cries of need.

It was as if they shared a body, and moved as one to the same rhythm, the same force that had compelled them to dance, and speak, and kiss. Don Diego, clearly practised in the art of love-making, seemed deeply affected, yet still retained some control, clearly seeking to give her, as he had promised, the most pleasure possible. Charlotte, however, was completely overwhelmed.

It was all she could not to scream very loudly as the amazing wave of pleasure overtook her again. Diego's approach to preventing her screams from waking the house was simply to kiss her, to swallow her screams as he drove her to greater heights.

Concepts like time meant nothing to Charlotte, she had no idea how long they moved, she was aware of nothing beyond the incredible sensations that Don Diego was giving her. For now, all she cared about was pleasure, and her Don. For now, all life beyond this bed could drift into nothing.

Her entire body throbbed and pulsed in time with his, until they came to a final, shuddering halt, as his release thundered through him, and he pulled himself from her at the last possible moment, as a gentleman should, in such a case.

They lay quiet, content to return to gently kissing and embracing each other, in what now felt like a very simple and plain manner, but which was comforting all the same.

*"Te amo Bueno, Charlotte, te amo"* he said, reverting to his native language. She had enough sense to have some idea of what he was saying, and she replied.

"Good heavens, Don Diego" she said "I seem to have fallen in love with you."

He held her in his arms tightly and planted a kiss on her forehead that would linger for the rest of the night.

He helped her to slide out of her dress, and leaving her underclothes and corset, slid her under the covers of the bed. She was still in too much of a haze to notice as he crept off, leaving her to drift into a pleasant, sensitive sleep from which she would awake a full-grown woman.

# Chapter Ten

The next day Charlotte Cavendish awoke to a strange and heady mixture of feelings. On one hand, she felt elated, buoyant, and ready for anything, gazing at the world with fresh eyes. She had made love to Don Diego and it had been the sweetest, most delectable experience of her entire life. This, she thought, with all the audacity that being young and infatuated can bring, is what life is really about. This is the inspiration for all the poetry, painting and music, the invisible force that drives people on to create and live freely. She wanted only to be held by Diego again, to feel him upon her, around her, inside her once more.

But, at the same time, a heaviness seemed to hang over the whole experience, and all of these new feelings. She had to frequently remind herself that she did not yet not know if his feelings were sincere.

Her own future sanity depended on her being practical now. If his feeling were not sincere, but last night had simply been a moment of inflamed passion, if this was all proved to be no more than a passing fancy it might leave her a bitter spinster, or the unhappy wife of some ageing Lord who did not mind her premarital indiscretions. She had not asked, dared not ask, about Anna-Maria, or told the Don about Hemsbridge, and his actions, the thought of which was still lingering on the edges of her consciousness like a mental fever.

It was possible that this passionate Argentine had merely used her, whispered sweet words to her to get her to open herself up to him and would then discard her in favour of his dark mistress back in his bedchamber, the one whom all the guests could not stop whispering about and inventing pasts for. It was horrible to contemplate the idea, but she knew that for now she must, and as long as she did she could not be entirely happy.

She was not certain what to do, but was quite certain that she must do something, very soon, to ascertain the truth. She deeply hoped that she had not been a complete little fool, overcome by desire, and ruined her future prospects. More than anything in the world, she wanted this to truly be love, and to be able to marry Don Diego.

Eschewing breakfast, she returned to the library. Her reasoning was twofold; that it was a peaceful and quiet space where she would not be bothered by the prattling of the remaining guests or easily stumbled upon by either Diego or Hemsbridge, and also because she had a strange urge to be there again, on the site of her passionate encounter with the Argentine Count.

It was as if, simply by being there in the flesh, the whole experience was made real and could be lived over and over again. She tried to focus on her book, the fourth volume of *The Life and Opinions of Tristram Shandy*, which she had been enjoying immensely, but she could not seem to clear space enough in her head to focus on more than a few sentences at a time. All she could think of was the kiss of Don Diego, his touch, his scent, his caress, tiny imprints of which all seemed to linger in the room, on the chaise longue, the books, even the floor, as well as on her skin. It was all very peculiar but she could not take her mind off any of it.

Then, once again without her initially realising, the door came open. Her heart fluttered uncontrollably for an instant, anticipating another magical encounter with the Don, but it was not his thick mane that came creeping through the doorframe but another one, ruddier in colour and more English in both disposition and complexion. Marquess Hemsbridge walked into the library, dressed in a vibrant scarlet coat that set off his flaming hair. He looked conspiratorial, as if he had many things to say to her.

"I thought I might find you here, Lady Charlotte" he said at once, striding towards the centre of the room. "- tales of your studiousness have, like rumours of your beauty, spread further afield than Derbyshire society. Pray tell, what is it you are reading?"

"Why sir, it is a volume of Laurence Stern's, which…" she eyed him for a moment, and then refocussed her attention on the book. She rather wished he would go away and leave her alone to her fantasies of another man "- incidentally, I would quite like to return to."

"Is that so? You wish to return to your saucy comedies of the last century, hardly a fit choice of reading material for a young lady of your standing, just as you wished so ardently to return to your Argentine rake last night."

"Sir!" she all but shrieked, shocked and saddened in equal measure by this latest impropriety. Would this young Marquess never cease in his improper lines of questioning?

Had he been so indulged for all of his privileged existence that he never saw fit to consider the feelings and perspectives of others? She had heard silly rumours about men with red hair and always dismissed them as old wives nonsense, but Hemsbridge seemed to be living proof that there was something to such tittle tattle.

"I've a good mind to report your filthy accusations to my father! He'll have you run off the Amfield estate before you can say 'unfit for high society'. Now state whatever business you feel you have with me and let us part more amicably than our present interaction."

To her surprise, he came closer to her rather than backing away from this critique. In fact she soon found that he was sitting on the chaise besides her, coming closer than she was comfortable with.

"Charlotte, I'll be frank with you…" he said

"- as if to suggest you have been anything else thus far!" her voice was heated.

He laughed lightly.

"You are correct of course. I have always been rather an impulsive man, quick to anger and jealousy. I just wanted to say that, I am sorry for what happened between us the other night, in the Italian garden. I have been thinking on it much since then and I…" he held her hand in his and she could feel that it was a little damp, indicating uneasiness. Perhaps at least, this demonstrated his sincerity. "- I think I might love you, Charlotte Cavendish." Immediately upon finishing this startling pronouncement, he started laying kisses on the side of her face, as if he expected her to immediately reciprocate.

A small part of her did feel like returning them. He was a handsome man, and she suspected he meant what he said, and was not using it simply as a pretext for a little rough wooing. But she could not, in all sincerity, return the favour. She still distrusted him, after their encounter the other night, and she had fallen very deeply into the heart and soul of another man. It would have been cruel to be anything but honest with him.

"I am sorry, My Lord" she said, as he continued to kiss her neck and then her cheek. "I am afraid I cannot say that I feel the same way in return. You see, I believe that I have fallen in love with another…" at this he sprang suddenly to his feet, moving with a renewed vigour that she found more than a little alarming.

"You hussy!" he exclaimed, looming over her. "I knew that you had been carousing with that Argentine rascal! How dare you deny your affections to a fellow countryman in favour of some dago! You know he has his mistress, whom he likely favours in the affairs of the flesh!"

"That is untrue, my Lord! How dare you impugn him, and call me such names.  This is beyond the pale!" she declared. She tried to get to her feet but Hemsbridge pushed her back down, and, before she knew what was happening or could muster any force with which to resist him, he had turned her around and was holding her down, against the chaise. She could feel him fidgeting with the frills and tassels on her skirts, his hands tangled in the decoration as he tried to work his way under her skirts, pushing them up, towards her more intimate areas. It was as if his actions of the other night were acceptable, and the fact that she had pulled away then and denied him access was irrelevant.

"I'm going to teach you a lesson in obedience to a man!" he said darkly, fidgeting with his own belt as he pressed her face hard into the chaise with the palm of his hand. She felt like crying out and screaming, and shrieked a little as she felt his hand clap stingingly into her buttocks. "If you are to go around consorting with Argentines you can only expect rough treatment thereafter, little Cavendish whore!" and though she struggled hard to wriggle out of his grasp and away from his aggressive, raw desire, he was strong. She was quite overwhelmed, and could only try to plead with him.

"No my lord, no!" she said, wincing at the thought of what she knew was to come. "You cannot! Think of my honour!"

"What honour?" he said with a maniacal grin. "You have none left, girl!"

"I don't know about that." Another voice spoke, from near the door, unmistakable, rich, Hispanic, Don Diego! *'Oh sweet day!'* thought Charlotte at once, he has come to my rescue!

"Don Diego!" she cried, with Hemsbridge's hand close to her throat, and her skirts tossed up onto her back, baring her buttocks, where the red imprint of Hemsbridge's hand stood out plainly. Liberation! She had been saved!

"What the devil are you doing here!" said Hemsbridge, desperately trying to put his breeches to rights and preparing to meet this intruder "Can you not see that the library is at present occupied?"

"I might very well ask you what you are doing here, my lord Hemsbridge" the Don said, moving implacably towards Charlotte and her assailant "- though I do not expect that, given the circumstances, I would receive an honest answer."

"You Argentine dog!" Hemsbridge cried, suddenly releasing Charlotte and lurching towards the Don.

Charlotte pulled herself up to sit on the couch, watching with horror as the two men came together in the middle of the room. Hemsbridge made to throw a punch, but Diego was too quick for him, and, using all of the agility he had honed back on the Pampas, threw himself out of the way of the oncoming blow. Then with an almighty crack, his fist connected with Hemsbridge's face, felling the English Marquess in a single blow.

"You fight like a damned coward!" Hemsbridge said from the floor, smearing his handkerchief with blood from his face, as he patted at his nose ineffectually.

"Do I indeed?" replied Diego, dusting his knuckles off from the impact. "I wasn't the one who had a lady pinned down beneath me against her will. What were you trying to do with her, recite the Psalter?"

"Cad!" was all Hemsbridge could think to say in response. Then, still on the floor, he turned himself to face in the direction of Charlotte. "He doesn't love you my lady, he's seduced you! He only wants you as a little respite from that exotic, flaunting mistress he's got up in his bedchamber!"

"How dare you sir!" now it was Don Diego's turn to be angry. "Is that what people have been saying of Anna-Maria? I am appalled at such a suggestion, the very thought!"

"Then who the hell is she? She doesn't look like a mother superior, and she doesn't dress like a chambermaid! Just who is this mysterious woman you're keeping up in your quarters?"

Charlotte looked up at the Don imploringly. Much as she resented him, Hemsbridge was articulating what she, and all the other guests for that matter, had desperately wanted to ask for the duration of Don Diego's stay at Amfield. What was the meaning of this Hernandez woman he was keeping with him, and, thought Charlotte, what relation was she to him?

"If you must know...." said Diego, fixing each of them in his gaze in turn, "... she is my younger sister, forced into a sudden exile by the revolution in our country, in which her husband was killed, and travelling under a pseudonym to avoid attracting the attention of those who betrayed him. We cannot yet be sure that the risk does not reach even here, but I will confess, her real name is Julia Fernanda Sanchez-Zapata, and I love her as dearly as any man could ever love a sibling. She is precious to me. She speaks not a word of English, and does not know this strange northern land. Even in June, the chill of the climate has given her a terrible fever which she is only now recovering from."

He spoke with such clarity, and such pain in his voice that neither Charlotte nor Hemsbridge could doubt for a second that he spoke the truth. The Englishman looked very sheepish, and made to rise to his feet and leave, forgetting for a moment the blood streaming from his nose, and his burning desire for Charlotte.

"If that is so, my Lord" he said, backing swiftly towards the door "- then I concede the field. My sincerest apologies to you both." He gave Charlotte a nervous little bow, and then scurried away.

He left Amfield later that afternoon without bothering to bid anyone a formal farewell, and would later send a letter of apology that would confuse Lord and Lady Derbyshire to no end.

"Is it true what he said?" said Diego, looking at Charlotte searchingly with his wide, dark eyes. "Have they been saying that Julia is my, as he said, mistress?"

Charlotte nodded gravely. She did not wish to bear bad news to this man ever, and now thought anything that might hurt him more evil than could possibly be imagined.

"I'm afraid it is, sir. There were some very outlandish rumours circulating, and I'm afraid I had no substantive arguments with which to pour scorn on them. I did not wish to believe it was true, but…"

He sat down beside her, swept her hand up in his, in a smooth movement, and kissed her fingers passionately.

"Oh *Santa Maria. Dios mio*, I can hardly believe it. To think that you thought I was merely seducing you, when in reality, my Lady...." He released her hand, and slid from the settee onto one knee before her. "I love you more fully than I have ever loved before, ever. It is rather, as you English say, rash of me to say this so early in our acquaintance and with no prior arrangement with your family, but, Charlotte...." he looked at her so hopefully that she almost wanted to weep and scream and burst out laughing all at once. Was this truly happening, to her?

"- will you marry me?"

"Oh yes, yes Don Diego."

The words came out of her not like words, but rather in the same way that tears or laughter sometimes force their own way out of someone by some natural process. She did not think about it, indeed she could not think at all in that moment, all her life was simply being lived, happening around her. There were no questions, there was only passion, and love.

"Of course I will marry you!"

"*Bueno*" he said, grabbing her and giving her a huge kiss. "Now let us find your father."

The very moment that Don Diego was proposing, old Lord Derbyshire (Stanley to his friends) was patiently putting up with an especially dull anecdote from Lady Frome. He could barely tolerate the company of his sister at the best of times, but this afternoon, over cream scones and tea in the drawing room, she was especially insufferable. Such a shame, he thought, that a happy occasion like a wedding required by convention the presence of one's relatives.

"… so I acquired a pair of otter-skin gloves from a Dutch merchant in London I happen to be acquainted with, a Mister Van Burren" she said, as undaunted by the yawns and glazed expressions of her audience as she ever was, "- but then I found that being a rather large-knuckled woman, I could not seem to fit my hand into them. So then I thought, ah! Herbie's got tiny little hands like a baby girl, haven't you Herbert?"

The esteemed Lord Frome saw fit only to nod at this remark. Whether or not he was happy to have his wife demeaning his hands so flagrantly in front of close friends and relatives he did not reveal.

"- so instead I saw fit to give them to him for the Grouse season, last winter. Kept the cold off awfully well, didn't they Herbie? You must see, he suffers in the colder months awfully, poor little chap, and they even saved him from some rather nasty burns when his firearm went off half-cocked, didn't they?" once again, Lord Herbert Frome could do no more than furnish a grave nod.

"Excellent, excellent to hear" said Lord Derbyshire, doing everything he could to be courteous to his guest. *'Will she never shut up?'* he was inwardly thinking.

Seconds later however, he was saved. A chorus of low gasps ran around the room, and faces suddenly trained on the doorway. Charlotte had entered, arm in arm with Don Diego. Every eye was trained on the pretty Cavendish daughter in a fine and elegant day dress, walking so closely with this handsome gentleman. There was a hush as they entered.

"Father…" Charlotte said immediately, bypassing conventional formality. She seemed a new, fresh person, brimming with happiness and confidence. Her hand was perched daintily on the arm of her Argentine, who was also beaming joy out at the room. "Don Diego and I have quite fallen in love!" There were smiles and 'ahh's' all around the room, followed by a short ripple of applause. Even the hardest-hearted of the guests found themselves able to do nothing but smile at the happy couple before them.

"'With your Lordship's permission" said Don Diego, striding forward as if he were taming a wild horse from the Pampas, "- I should like to take Miss Charlotte's hand in marriage."

"Another wedding?" boomed Lord Derbyshire in pretend horror.

"Are you girls conspiring to drive me into debtors' prison?" everyone laughed. They all knew that the Cavendish family could easily afford two of the finest weddings of the social season.

"I jest, of course, I give you my blessing. Of course you may marry!"

Once again the drawing room was filled with cheers. Even the oldest and most grizzled servants present would have to concede that they had never witnessed a happier scene in all their years at Amfield House.

Everyone's hearts swelled with pride and joy at the young love that they had witnessed blossoming this afternoon.

"You shall have to brush up a little on your Spanish, my dear!" said Lord Derbyshire, more full of mirth than anyone else.

"I hear these Argentine types are little interested in the English tongue!"

"That will not be necessary, my Lord" said Don Diego. "I have recently acquired property in your fair county of Buckinghamshire, which I intend to make my permanent residence. I have always had a great love for your country, a love which will now find its greatest expression in my wedding to Charlotte".

"Well then" said the Earl, grinning "-everything seems to have worked itself out quite nicely." And he turned around to face all of his assembled guests, and led them in a hearty three cheers.

# The End

**(You'll find a taste of book 5, "The Rake's Unlikely Redemption" just after the 'About the Author' section in this book!)**

Arietta Richmond
Regency Historical Romance

Arietta Richmond has been a compulsive reader and writer all her life. Whilst her reading has covered an enormous range of topics, history has always fascinated her, and historical novels been amongst her favourite reading.

She has written a wide range of work, from business articles and other non-fiction works (published under a pen name) but fiction has always been a major part of her life. Now, her Regency Historical Romance books are finally being released. The Derbyshire Set is comprised of 10 shorter novels (6 released so far). The 'His Majesty's Hounds' series is comprised of 10 novels, with the fifth having just been released.

She also has a standalone longer novel shortly to be released, and two other series of novels in development.

She lives in Australia, and when not reading or writing, likes to travel, and to see in person the places where history happened.

Be the first to know about it when Arietta's next book is released!

Sign up to Arietta's newsletter at

http://www.ariettarichmond.com

When you do, you will receive a free copy of the <u>subscriber exclusive</u> novella **'A Gift of Love',** a prequel to the Derbyshire Set series, which ends on the day that 'The Earl's Unexpected Bride' begins

This story is not for sale anywhere – it is absolutely exclusive to newsletter subscribers!

# Other Books in 'The Derbyshire Set'

Available at all good book stores and for ebook readers too!

Coming Soon!

# Here is your preview of the next book in 'The Derbyshire Set' by Arietta Richmond

# The Derbyshire Set ~ Book 5

# Regency Historical Romance

# The Rakes Unlikely Redemption

# Arietta Richmond

# Chapter One

The glass slipped through his fingers, clipped the polished timber arm of the chair, and shattered. Whisky splashed - onto his elegant trousers, and his priceless Chinese rug.  He cursed, half-heartedly, then simply sat there, brooding darkly.

Drinking didn't ease the pain and James Blackwood knew this. This did not stop him however, and had not stopped him once during the past twelve years of hard living. Really there was nothing at all that did seem to ease the pain, but he carried on, drinking and smoking, and gambling and womanizing, travelling the world, hunting and hosting the orgiastic parties for which he had become notorious.

To any outside observer it might have seemed like a fascinating existence, exciting, glamorous even, a life defined by freedom and adventure.

To Blackwood himself though, it had become boring, outstandingly dull, dry, a routine, and also a burden. He dragged an awful reputation with him and attracted the wrong sorts of people.

Where once he had enjoyed the dark and dangerous reputation that he had created, and the horrified, yet fascinated responses that it aroused in women, now it was tedious – he no longer wished to live up to the reputation that he had created for himself.

His manner of life had not made him happy for years, if indeed it ever had, and yet he carried on, seemingly unable to change even as it became more and more inappropriate and difficult as he got older.

He had drunk a lot in the past few weeks. Events at Amfield House he felt, had forced him to do so, or at least given him enough of an excuse that he was able to look at his ageing face in the mirror every morning and blame someone else.

He was still compellingly handsome in a dark, mysterious way and he knew this, though he was only thirty –two, he felt the press of old age slowly creeping in upon him and, in the back of his mind, he knew that his days as a serial seducer might soon be behind him.

Around the county balls and the marriage markets of high society, young ladies might be a little less concerned by a gentleman's age, looks, or virginal status than gentlemen were by those attributes in ladies, but this did not mean that any pretty young miss was willing to hitch up her petticoats for some old cad just because he had a twinkle in his eye and an intriguing reputation.

Like any other man about town, he had relied on his appearance at least as much as he had as on his aura of fascination and wry charm, his thick dark hair and gold flecked chestnut eyes that glistened in the candlelight, his firm jawline that shadows seemed to cling to, his penchant for the latest London fashions in dress.

If he carried on like this however, all that would fade away and he would be left an aging bachelor, with nothing, slowly drinking and gambling himself to death, unable to exert the sort of power he had once had over women, with only his servants and a dwindling circle of friends for company.

At least that was his fear, in the dark hours of the night, when he could not sleep, but had no distractions left to draw upon.

So many of Blackwood's friends had abandoned him over the years that he had lost count, and certainly he had lost any contact with most who might once have had a care for him. A few of course, he had rather actively fallen out with - Jenkinson had challenged him to a duel, only to flee to America at the last minute, to escape the possibility of an honourable death, and Manninghorn had retired to his obscure estate in Ireland, after Blackwood had positively run him out of town over gambling debts.

Many of them had married, and quit the rakish life of late-night carousing and whoring, which they had enjoyed (or at least, indulged in) with Blackwood. They had drifted away, to settle down to a life of domestic respectability, somewhere in the provinces. One such man, Henley, who had inherited a well-endowed Viscountcy, had even taken the trouble of writing a stern letter to him.

The self-righteous insistence presented in that letter, that Henley had enjoyed their companionship, but that they must never see each other again, now that he was living in rural Berkshire with a child on the way and a household to maintain, was rather galling, if also darkly amusing. Another, Denverton, had pulled Blackwood aside and threatened him with violence after he had felt that his former drinking associate was flirting rather too insistently with his fiancée. He was not wrong, Blackwood thought with a dark smile, although this abrupt termination of friendships brought him no joy now.

Around the great houses of England, James Blackwood's name was mostly disgraced, and few well-intentioned and respectable parents were naïve enough to let him anywhere near their daughters.

When you counted in those who had died- Illingford from a fever contracted in the West Indies, Newbury in a shipwreck in the Bay of Biscay, and even a number killed in the war, Blackwood had few he could call on for support. Three of those whom he could generally count on were here today, in his London townhouse, helping him to work his way through several bottles of Scotch, and at least as many again of Port.

There was Tomlinson, a tall and fresh-faced gentleman who did not look his thirty-four years, the youngest son of the Earl of Sussex. He had disgraced himself having an affair with a chambermaid, been disinherited by his father, and now lived off a modest allowance and a few investments. Likewise Cranston, who had spent time in a Lancashire jail for duelling and now lived largely by gambling, spending wildly when he was in luck, leaning heavily on acquaintances when he was out of it.

And then there was Travers, Blackwood's protégé, a confirmed bachelor for life and a hard-living Marquess who spent about as much time on his country estate in Cornwall as he did on the surface of the moon. Over the years, Travers had frittered away most of his considerable fortune keeping up with Blackwood, running around London society seducing young ladies, holding lavish parties in his Mayfair townhouse, and betting hundreds of guineas on single horse races. Of all his friends, Travers was probably the closest, but they were ageing together with little dignity, and in both their cases the money was starting to run out.

This unfortunate financial situation had not, however, prevented the four of them from passing a raucous afternoon at Epsom racecourse for the annual Derby Stakes. It was one of the premier occasions of the London social calendar, a chance for well-bred (and not so well-bred!) young ladies and gentlemen to see and be seen, meet potential spouses and reinforce their place in high society. The young ladies had been radiant, the drink plentiful, and the horses as fast and daring as ever. It had been a perfect occasion for Blackwood and his companions.

"-Good god sir! That final furlong!" exclaimed Cranston, ignoring the broken glass and continuing as if nothing had happened, recalling memories of a few hours past. "... Damned if I've ever seen a runner come back like that! He was going like the clappers, incredible!"

"It would have been considerably more impressive..." said Travers, interjecting "... had any of us had the good sense to actually back the accursed horse. What was his name, Busby, or something?"

"Damned stupid name for a racehorse if ever I heard one" Cranston cut in "When was the last time you heard of a 50 to 1 outsider winning the Derby? When for that matter, was a 50 to 1 outsider even running in the Derby? I smell foul play, some rake has had us all for fools."

"Not that you ever seem to have the good sense to back the right horse, my good man" replied Travers. "I feel your case would be somewhat stronger if you had a record for managing anything but haemorrhaging guineas like you'd contracted a nasty fever and they were dropping out of your bowels"

"A charming image" said Tomlinson, sarcastically, smoking a fat cigar as he leant back in his chair with his feet resting on the table. "You're not quite as bad as Jimmy here though…"

Some of Blackwood's acquaintances called him Jimmy. It didn't yet annoy him quite enough for him to tell them to stop.

"- backs the wrong bloody horse all the damned time! Not just at the races mind!" the other three men laughed raucously.

Blackwood had the decency to smile, but tonight these jibes hurt more than usual. They had all heard by now about the situation at Amfield, how he had been rejected by Blanchette Cavendish and disgraced in a duel by a Captain of the Guards. It seemed that all of high society had heard something of the unfortunate affair, and his so-called friends were determined not to let any of it rest.

"What was her excuse this time, Jimmy old boy? Had to pop off to see her aunt about a lapdog? Or maybe sick of having one hanging around all the time and asking for someone to get rid of it!" they all laughed again, most pointedly at him.

If only they knew, he thought, about the seduction in the library, then they'd think twice before comparing him to a damned lapdog. He tried to muster a witty response but was too drunk, too tired, and, if truth be told, too depressed, to manage.

"I will remind you, Jeremiah Tomlinson, that you are a guest in my house, and I can just as soon have you ejected as have you sit here drinking my best whisky and resting your filthy boots on my table!"

"Oof, touched a nerve have we?" Tomlinson reacted sarcastically. "... cheer up Jim, not the end of the world! You only lost, what, forty guineas and all of your honour?" More laughter, and this time Blackwood felt it as a body blow. He could not stand it any longer, this inane, manly banter, this mockery of his honour. All he wanted was for these three imbeciles to leave him in peace.

"Forty, as opposed to your sixty-five, and at least I can afford it!" genuine anger strayed into his voice.

"Steady on old chap!" Tomlinson blurted in response. "What are you going to do? Challenge me to a duel and then miss wildly? I can tell you, I might not have the same sense of mercy as that blustering Captain! I might actually have to shoot you for that particular remark!"

Something snapped inside – James could feel it, almost a physical release of long dammed pressure. "Get out of my damned house you dog!" He could not contain himself "... if you want to speak to me like that, you can buy your own bloody drinks, go!"

Drink had suppressed all inhibition and sorrow had stifled any wit or charm. He wanted nothing more than to wrap his hands around Tomlinson's neck and wring all life out of him, but he could not summon the energy. Instead, he hauled himself to his feet, a little unsteadily, but with as much dignity as he could muster, flung the door to his drawing room open, and gestured forcefully for them all to leave. Tomlinson and Cranston looked sheepish as they left, but Travers, to whom he was far closer, gave him a knowing wink, before skulking off with the other pair into the London night.

Blackwood sank into his chair, took another glass, poured himself more whisky, and lit up a cigarillo. As so often happened, when he was in low spirits and alone, his thoughts turned to Honour. *'What a strange sort of curse it is'* he thought to himself *'that my dear lost love shares her name with a virtue I shall never possess.'* There was a cynical edge to his thought, as he reminded himself, again, that in reality, she had been just as much of an uncaring, self-serving whore as most women were, when it came down to it. Whatever she had said to him when they were together, she had been quick enough to up and marry some old man with money.

It had all been such a cruel twist of fate. He had met her, his dream, his ideal, the woman who could have saved him from this messy and sordid existence, when he was too young, too shy, too foolish to take advantage. Honour had astounded him with her beauty, her wit, her bearing, her whole manner of assurance and grace, but it seemed that her words had been lies, that she had not shared his feelings, and she had gone off to marry some rich old man of whom her father approved.

Nothing had ever really gone Blackwood's way since, despite all of the short-lived affairs and decadent parties. He could never be happy as long as there was a hole in his heart that, perhaps, he almost admitted to himself in the depths of his darkest moments, only she could fill. '*Maudlin rubbish*' he thought to himself sternly, '*no woman is worth it – I should thank her for showing me early what selfish whores all women are*'. He internally congratulated himself on the accuracy of this belief, noting that Blanchette had, after all, just proved its truth to him, yet again.

Taking another sip of his whisky, he steadfastly repressed the little niggle of doubt that scratched at the edge of his thinking, and leant back in the chair. But no matter what stern thoughts, the image of Honour's face would not leave his mind. He sat back in his chair, sighed, and let a single silver tear trickle down his face. '*Life*' he thought heavily '*life, life, life…*'

# Chapter Two

"Oh Sissy!" exclaimed Beatrice, flicking her sandy hair idly like a girl of almost twenty years should only ever allow herself to do on special occasions.

"- will there be music, and dancing there tonight?" Honour could barely contain a heavy sigh and a frown at her younger sister's inane remarks. She had fielded questions of this nature all afternoon and was, by now, quite sick and tired of them. Her own adolescent enthusiasm for occasions such as that at the house of the Duke of Uxbridge, which they were planning to attend tonight, was now so distant that she could barely remember it.

Those lingering days of anticipation, the scent of powder and perfume as one gets ready, feeling the nerves in one's stomach as the maid pulled pinned and tucked into place the bodice of your best new frock.

Such notions Honour might have recalled had she been in the mood for sentiment. Beatrice however, had crushed such sentimentality, with her incessant wittering.

"…and will there be" Sissy paused heavily at the word "-gentlemen present?"

"Yes, Beatrice, there will be. Unless that is, one of them hears you calling me 'sissy' and rushes off in horror at the thought of a silly little girl being in attendance at an occasion that is strictly reserved for grown-ups."

It almost hurt her to see Beatrice's sweet and serene face gradually turn more worried at her stern words, but she had endured enough today, and in the carriage on their way up from the country. It was time for a little sisterly revenge, so she went on –

"For there will also be punch there, and stronger drinks as well I'll wager, at least for the gentlemen. The eldest amongst them will want to discuss hunting, and cricket, and the derby stakes, and the best way to polish off a winged grouse - and the thought of giggling young girls will make them most displeased, and quite possibly a little vexed."

"Oh Honour, I cannot help it! I am just so happy to be in London at my first ball, I feel as if…" Beatrice paused a moment, looking for just the right words "… as if, were an especially powerful wind to come along, it would sweep me into the air by me petticoats!"

"Let us hope that no such occurrence comes to pass," Honour replied, maintaining her sternness, "- such a thing would be quite improper and I imagine people would talk."

*'And aside from that',* Honour thought to herself, uncharitably. *'It shall be my role tonight to ensure that no hyperactive young buck with a head full of the wrong sorts of ideas comes along and sweeps you off by your petticoats either...'*

Tonight Honour was to be a chaperone. For the first time in her life she had crossed the threshold. She had moved from willing young ewe, protected from the wolves on the perimeter of the flock, to the role of shepherdess, silently warding them off. Time had permanently changed her role, as it changes all things, and there was nothing to be done about it.

She looked at Beatrice with a strange mixture of yearning and envy. Never again would she be filled with such giddy feeling and innocent ideas, never again would she have to have an older relative beat aside handsome and willing suitors. It all saddened her too much, and she had no desire to go out to the ball tonight, or to endlessly hear of it from Beatrice.

Yet she had agreed to do just that.

Beatrice was Honour's sister. She had a brother as well, who, at thirty-one, was a year older than her and a commodore in the Royal Navy. She had grown up with him, Richard, grown used to his every frown and stench and passing fancy as only a sibling can, resenting and loving and ignoring him in equal measure. She had not, which the distance in their respective ages bore witness to, grown up with Beatrice. Beatrice had come later, twelve whole years later, by which time she and Richard were virtually adults (or so they thought!) and Beatrice was no more than a bawling swaddle of cloth for a nanny to take care of and for their mother to dote on.

There had been rumours around the estate, and whispered more quietly in the *ton* of course. There always are, when a rich and well-bred woman births a child some years after her first brood have passed into adolescence. She was still just about fecund enough to plausibly manage it, but it seemed, to many onlookers, unlikely that the child had been sired by Sir Danvers Wormsley, their father. He had long since retreated into eccentricity and distance.

Beatrice was generally whispered of as the product of an affair, likely between her mother and a stable lad. It was a strange thought that had permanently distanced Beatrice from their family and community, although, being a naïve and self-contained girl, she had barely noticed the scorn her very existence had attracted.

Honour had never managed to love Beatrice. She could pity her, sympathise with her strange existence - shut up in a cold country house with two ageing parents and a small staff - but love would have been far too heavy a label for any such feelings to bear the weight of. They had never been close, and had shared few of life's milestones in each other's company.

Before Beatrice was seven, Honour had been sent off to marry in any case. The Wormsleys had never been rich, but they had good pedigree and when a suitable man, the ageing Baron Fotherington, had taken a shine to Honour's red hair and easily vivacious nature, the match had been made and that had been that. She was given no choice, and the fact that she loved another was of no concern to her father.

The sisters parted company, seemingly forever, reunited briefly only on special family occasions and when an obscure relative had had the temerity to die.

Like her relationship with her sister, Honour's career attending balls had also been ended by her marriage to the Baron. He had doted on her, allowing her space, time to adjust to the life of a wife and then, hopefully, eventually mother, not minded her friendships with the servants, her greater interest in reading racy novels than in conversing with him, and even the affair she carried on, discreetly, with one of the serving boys (a groom called Rogers closer to her own age) in her second year as his wife. As long as she shared his bed, called him 'my darling' and kissed him on the cheek every night, the old man had been happy.

He was too fat and aged to sire any heirs, and despite (or perhaps because) of this, they grew to be relatively happy together.  She did, however, always wonder what would have happened if she had been able to marry James instead.  But he had, it seemed, not felt her loss too badly, as he had gone off overseas within a short time after her marriage, and not come back for years.  So perhaps, she told herself, she was better off without him.

Now though, Honour was a widow, of nearly two years, and widows need something to fill their days. She could not bring herself to sit at home all day, commanding her servants like an admiral on his quarterdeck, or re-reading the same limited selection of volumes, which Fotherington had provided for her. So now, at her own mother's insistence, and to her little sister's eternal delight, she was sponsoring Beatrice's entrance into society, taking her out to find the charming, eligible young suitor that she herself had been denied. There was a cruel irony to the entire enterprise, but then Honour supposed, that's life. No-one chooses their fate any more than they choose their station in society or the colour of their eyes.

"I cannot bring myself to take a final decision, Sissy!" Beatrice declared suddenly, after passing several minutes making vague pirouettes all over the drawing room floor, one dress or another held up against her.

"Should I wear the blue one, or the yellow one?" Beatrice glared at the frocks she had picked out for the evening, now lying on the bed where she had abandoned them, as if it were somehow their fault that she could not decide. Both were more than pretty, and elegant as far as Honour was concerned, and both had been paid for out of her late husband's generous endowment. Beatrice, 'little Sissy', as she liked to be called, knew nothing of such matters. As far as she was concerned, they might as well have materialised out of thin air, for her and her alone.

"I do not know, Bea" Honour said, allowing the affection she had somewhere deep inside her for her sister to come up, if only for a second. "I cannot possibly choose it for you. You must make your own decisions in these matters henceforth, if you are to be a lady of society. Discernment is most attractive in a woman." Beatrice gazed whimsically up at the white rococo ceiling. Up there, above the plaster, and the roof, and then eventually the clouds, there seemed to her to be a heavenly realm where every dream comes true and all gentlemen are decent, willing, and above all dashed good-looking. To get to it, all she needed to do was pick the right dress, but the effort of the decision was so much that it caused her to screw up her face and dither for what felt like an age. 'If only' Honour thought '*the most momentous decision of my life had simply been over a damned frock*'. She kept these words to herself, and allowed Beatrice to keep her illusions.

"I think I shall wear the blue one" she said at last, with all the finality of a Roman Emperor. "It matches my eyes best."

"A very fine choice, my dear. The blue one it shall be".

Honour stood, and called for the maid to assist Beatrice with dressing for her first grand ball.

"Now I must go and prepare as well. Do try to sit still for Mary to dress your hair Sissy."

As Honour swept from the room, she wondered idly who she would see at the ball, what old acquaintance might be renewed, and what she might find to relieve the boredom of a life with no real direction.

Get

# "The Rake's Unlikely Redemption"

as soon as it's released – go to
http://www.ariettarichmond.com

and make sure that you are signed up for news and release notices !

# Books in the 'His Majesty's Hounds' Series

Redeeming the Marquess (coming soon)

Healing Lord Barton (coming soon)

Winning the Merchant Earl (coming soon)

Loving the Bitter Baron (coming soon)

Rescuing the Countess (coming soon)

Attracting the Spymaster (coming soon)

# Other Books from Dreamstone Publishing

Dreamstone publishes books in a wide variety of categories – here are some of our other bestselling books:-

We have books in many categories, ranging from Erotica and Romance to Kids Books, Books on Writing, Business Books, Photography, Cook Books, Diaries, Coloring books and much more. New books are released each month.

Be the first to know when our next books are coming out

Be first to get all the news – sign up for our newsletter at

http://www.dreamstonepublishing.com

www.ingramcontent.com/pod-product-compliance
Lightning Source LLC
Chambersburg PA
CBHW071834190726
48292CB00005B/1775